I0562470

PASSION2RIGHT PRESENTS

Loyal Snakes

2

Skeet's Pride

By Rosa James

Contact Information:

Email: misuselsnake@gmail.com

Website: Passion2Right.com

@2023 Rosa James

Cover Art by: Bear-man/shutterstock.com, OSTILLisFrank Cambi/shutterstock.com, Certain stock imagery Getty Images

Varga Woo/shutterstock.com

Edited by Chanekka Pullens

Published by Passion2Right 07/30 /2023

ISBN: 979-8-218-24852-9

Books may be purchased in quantity and/or special sales by contacting the author by email at: misuselsnake@gmail.com, with 'Book Purchase' in the subject line.

Because of the dynamic nature of the Internet, any web addresses, or links contained in this book may have changed since publication and may no longer be valid.

1. *Fiction Fantasy*
2. *Erotic*

Printed in the USA

Chapter 1   Captivity

Chapter 2   Rescue Me

Chapter 3   Vengeful Envy

Chapter 4   Where Is Jay

Chapter 5   Priest and Donavan

Chapter 6   Homecoming

Chapter 7   Reunited

Chapter 8   New Beginnings

Chapter 9   The Beginning Of The End

Chapter 10   The Hunt

Chapter 11   Goodbye Yasmine

Chapter 12   Honor Thy Mother

Chapter 13   Partners In Crime

Chapter 14   SWAMP

Chapter 15   Breaking Point

Chapter 16   Desperate Love

Chapter 17   Dysfunction

Chapter 18   Seven Months Later

Chapter 19   Out The Box

Chapter 20   Dorlinda

Chapter 21   Business As Usual

Chapter 22   Escapade

Chapter 23   Tranquility

Chapter 24   Reveal

Chapter 25   Goodbye Baton City

Chapter 26   Rhodium Tag

Chapter 27   See No Evil, Hear No Evil, Speak No Evil

Chapter 28   Angel of Darkness

Warning

This book contains fictional events that involve sex, violence, death, and inappropriate language.

Please proceed with caution.

CAPTIVITY

In the damp concrete cell, Rena laid on the dingy mattress in the darkness listening to the roaring sound of the Atlantic Ocean. The serene sound of the water took her mind off her offensive body odor. She had not showered since she was abducted.

Every night as she lay in the cell, she thought about her last night of freedom. That night was filled with trauma when her mother Yasmine came home intoxicated and shot her cousin Rachel. Rena ran for her life afraid that her mother would turn the gun on her next. She ran to multiple neighbors' homes beating on the door and no one answered. Everyone was used to Yasmine's shenanigans and would normally help Rena when she was in need. However, after Yasmine pulled a gun on one of the neighbors, word got around to stay out of it.

As Rena's bare feet slapped the damp pavement, she looked around hoping to see a police car. For hours, the seventeen-year-old wandered the streets trying to figure out what she should do next. With no luck, she decided to go to a police station. As she walked, she thought about Rachel lying on the living room floor bleeding out. She knew her cousin was dead because there was so much blood. She began to cry. Why would her mother do such a thing?

Just when things could not get worse, a black van drove alongside her. When it came to a complete stop, two men jumped out of the back and grabbed her. Rena tried to fight to get away from the men. Inside the van she was tied up, mouth covered with duct tape, and blind folded.

Rena estimated that at least three weeks had passed since her abduction. She considered it a new day when the metal tray slid under the door containing cornbread, and a plastic pouch of water. Despite the poor living conditions, Rena was thankful for the tiny window that offered a beam of light throughout the day, the working toilet, a chair, and a mattress to sleep on.

Her thoughts were interrupted by someone entering the room. She did not need light to know who it was. It was the same man that had been coming to her room every day since she arrived. When she heard the squeak of the chair as he sat, she stood up and began dancing seductively while sauntering over to him. The man's only word was "dance". She pondered why because they were in the darkness, he could barely see her. She wondered what he looked like. The only recognition was that he always wore the same cologne.

He kept his visits short and never touched her. Was this his plan for the rest of her life? This mysterious man visiting her for a short time and making her dance in the dark. No torture, no shower, just cornbread and water. To Rena, the thought of repeating this every night for the rest of her life drove her crazy. She hoped at some point her body odor would become so offensive, that he would allow her to at least shower.

A half hour later, the man left the room leaving her alone again. Rena flopped back down on the mattress and continued staring into the darkness as she listened to the waves.

When Kyle stepped into his living room, his sister Janice sat enjoying a drink as she admired the view of the ocean in the darkness. When she turned and saw him, she hurried over and gave him a warm greeting, "I have missed you. How is the gift I sent you working out?"

Once she released him from the embrace, Kyle spoke, "Oh, sacred sister, she is beautiful. I appreciate you and all your efforts to make me happy after what happened. But it will never replace what..." he paused. It was painful to speak about his castration. The thought of living and not being able to feel the inside of a woman or have children made Kyle wish Skeet and Daubs would have just killed him.

Janice empathized with her brother. "I am so sorry about what happened to you. But just think, you have his daughter and can do whatever you want with her." Her voice was both sincere and sinister.

Kyle did not offer a response. He knew Janice was trying to make things better, but she had no idea the ramification of how he felt. He was a man and the greatest definition of that was taken away. He would never feel whole again. He resented God for not allowing him to bleed to death. Day by day, his mental stability was crumbling, and he knew that ultimately, he would kill Rena and then take his own life.

RESCUE ME

On San Lucas Mountain, Lada used her binoculars to watch Kyle's place. She spent five days conducting surveillance on Kyle's routine and who was coming or going. She tried to zero in to get a better look at Janice but the sombrero she wore concealed most of her face.

The American government made a deal with her. She could continue her businesses in the United States if she killed Kyle, who was a former CIA agent fired because he went rouge.

Once Janice made her exit, Lada waited for Kyle to go to bed before she made her move. She traveled by boat to the edge of his private beach. Once she gave the signal, the agents disable the security system. She put on her night vision glasses and went inside the house moving quietly. She spent countless hours studying the floorplan, so she knew where everything was including the hidden cellar. When she arrived at Kyle's bedroom suite, she found him asleep.

Lada eased towards the bed with her gun drawn. When she was close enough, she aimed for Kyle's chest and pulled the trigger three times. She confirmed her target deceased before going to the cellar. When she made it below the house, she was mortified to find that Kyle had many children locked in cells. She used a key to release the master lock opening the cells. The children began to cautiously come out. When they saw Lada, she gave them the okay to go up the stairs. She then noticed that only one door did not open. She approached the door and began examining the lock. She went through her supplies to retrieve her universal key. When the door opened, Lada could see Rena was standing in the corner of the room.

"You're free," she spoke before turning and walking away.

Rena hurried out of the cell and followed her. When they reached the top level, there were children running around rummaging through the kitchen cabinets for food and water while agents tried to gain control of them.

"Bring a bus. There's a house full of children!" yelled one of the agents over the walkie-talkie.

Lada went out the back door heading to her boat. Her job was finally finished, and she could return home to her husband. When she made it to her boat, she heard a noise causing her to turn quickly aiming her gun. When she saw it was Rena, she put her gun away and gave her a questioning look before speaking, "Young lady, you are free to go wherever you want."

"I know, but where am I?" questioned Rena. Lada took a better look at the girl and knew she did not belong in Mexico. "You are in Cabo, Mexico."

"Ma'am, I am not from here. I live in the United States," said Rena. Lada gestured for her to get on the boat.

They sailed for twenty minutes to Lada's lavish yacht that was waiting. Lada pressed a button on her watch and the side of the yacht opened allowing the boat to enter. Once inside, the first thing Lada did was show her the shower. Grateful, Rena showered until there was no more hot water. She exited the narrow bathroom and into a bedroom where some clothing awaited on the bed. Rena took a seat on the bed; it was soft, and she looked forward to getting some good sleep on it. She could smell the aroma of food, so she dressed quickly while observing the various photos on the wall. Her smile changed to confusion when she saw a photo of her cousin Rachel's father Skeet.

"How does she know Skeet?" Rena questioned herself.

"You know Skeet?" questioned Lada, standing in the doorway.

Rena jumped while answering, "Yes, he is my cousin Rachel's father."

"Let's talk more over a hot meal," said Lada, gesturing for her to follow.

When they entered the kitchen area, Rena took a seat as Lada prepared her food. "I hope you like cabbage soup," said Lada, placing two bowls on the table and taking a seat across from Rena who dug in not offering a response. Lada let her get a few bites in before inquiring, "Skeet is your cousin Rachel's father. So how did you end up at Kyle's place?"

Rena looked up briefly and answered, "I was abducted over three weeks ago."   "What happened the day you were taken?" Lada questioned.

"My mother shot Rachel and I ran out the house to get help. I began walking to the closest police station when I got abducted and they brought me here," answered Rena.

"When your mother shot Rachel, did she die?" questioned Lada.

Rena dropped her spoon into the bowl and cradled her head while speaking, "She was bleeding a lot and not moving. I think so." She began to cry.

Lada took a deep breath before assuring Rena that everything would be okay. She instructed her to eat as much as she wanted before getting some sleep.

When Rena was in a deep sleep, Lada contacted Borya who was waiting for her call. "Mother! Glad to hear from you. I saw the news. It appears that the CIA was finally able to get over to Mexico to get Kyle." Lada checked to make sure Rena was still asleep before responding, "Yeah, he deserved whatever he got. That man was sick."

"Very true. The news reported children being held captive. Was that true?" asked Borya.

"Saw it with my own eyes. Made me think about when I was held captive at a very young age," responded Lada.

"When are you coming home? Father is worrying himself sick."

"Very soon. It is time to reunite with your brother now that the government is off my ass. Tell your father to prepare something nice for dinner tomorrow. I am bringing a guest that you will find interesting," finished Lada before ending the call. Lada took a shot of vodka before turning in for the night. She would wake up at sunrise and head back home with plans to reunite with her son.

Baton City Hospital

The next morning, Skeet and Clarissa sat inside the conference room waiting for the doctor. Rachel had been in a coma since the night she was shot, and Yasmine was nowhere to be found. Everyone was so consumed with Rachel, they did not notice that Rena was missing.

Clarissa looked over at Skeet who had not said anything to her. She knew it was because she broke her promise to keep their daughter safe after she was raped by her brother-in-law years ago. Relocating to Texas to start a new life, Clarissa vowed to never return to Baton City. She later had her daughter Ebony and was going to get married, but she relapsed and was back on drugs and alcohol. She ended up getting into some trouble in Texas, so she sent Ebony to live with her father and took Rachel back to Baton City.

The doctor entered. He greeted them before taking a seat at the head of the conference table. "Skeet and Clarissa, I am sorry, but Rachel has not showed any brain activity since she arrived at the hospital. It has been almost four weeks. Unfortunately, it's our policy to remove her from all life sustaining machines in forty-eight hours and allow her to transition," the doctor explained.

Frantic, Clarissa fell out of her chair onto the floor and began crying. The doctor peeked out the door and gestured for a couple nurses to come inside the room to help her. However, her crying turned to rage when she looked up at Skeet who was still sitting in his chair calm. "You're just going to sit there and let them kill our daughter! Do something!" she yelled.

Skeet took a deep breath and tried to choose his words before speaking, "Clarissa, I hate to say this, but you are the one that killed our daughter. I knew this day would come, that's why I suggested she live with me. But you wanted control and to get back at me for marrying Janay. Now you want me to do something. This would never have happened if Rachel had been with me from day one. Clarissa, you know how much I love my daughter and I would kill anyone or anything about her. So never question my reactions to anything. Besides, someone must keep their head on straight because all you are going to do is use this to get sympathy from everyone. So don't worry, I will handle my daughter's final arrangements. Because I am sure that when you leave this hospital, you will be at the first liquor store and drug house numbing the pain." He exited the conference room.

The doctor instructed the nurses to keep an eye on Clarissa while he headed to his office where Skeet was waiting. When the doctor closed the door and took a seat, Skeet handed him an envelope full of money.

"Thanks for your assistance in this matter. I completed all the necessary forms. You will receive the rest of your money when Rachel is pronounced dead. Once you call it, no one is to have access to see her but me."

When the doctor nodded, Skeet stood up and exited the office. He returned to Rachel's room where Clarissa was sitting in the window seal looking out at the cloudy sky. He turned to leave not wanting to be in the same room with her, but she stopped him.

"Remember the good times we shared. Skeet, what happened to us? We had a family. Now we can't even come together at a time like this."

Her words infuriated him. Here she was acting oblivious to the fact she was the one who ruined the relationship. Skeet would never forget the grievous feeling of coming back to an empty home to find a "Dear John letter". He would never reveal to her how hurt he was and the challenges it had been for him to find a woman who could fill the empty pit she left in his heart. The fact was that Clarissa's issues outweighed her beauty and love. Moral to the story, some things are just not good for you no matter how beautiful they appear or how good they make you feel.

"Clarissa, enough with the drama filled behavior. Don't try to use this situation to rekindle anything between us. What you can do is lead me to Yasmine because she must pay for this."

"Oh, don't worry I am going to find that bitch. But I just want you to know that I apologize from the bottom of my heart for any pain I have caused you. You have full control over Rachel's final affairs. Please, just give my daughter an honorable homegoing ceremony and you won't hear another peep out of me."

Skeet nodded and exited the hospital room leaving Clarissa. He got on the elevator and as he rode, he took a trip down memory lane. The partying, drinking, and drugs was more important than love and family to Clarissa. When times were good, she had him on cloud nine, but when they were bad, it was like dealing with a hangover. Skeet needed to sever the ties between he and the woman that broke his heart and the only way to move on would be Rachel's death.

VENGEFUL ENVY

For weeks, Yasmine managed to stay hidden from everyone except for Clarissa who spotted her in front of a known drug house. The lack of personal care had her looking a mess from head to toe. Her hair was matted, clothing was dingy, and her shoes were worn. Sloppy drunk, Yasmine did not notice her sister approaching. This confrontation would be the worst between the sisters.

Once in arms reach, Clarissa grabbed her sister and began punching her. Yasmine took every blow without fighting back because she knew she deserved it. "You bitch! You killed my daughter!" Clarissa screamed, landing punches.

All the hustlers hanging around kept their distance, not wanting to get involved except for Ken. He instructed one of his boys to go get Don, Clarissa and Yasmine's cousin. Seconds later, Don strutted out of the house and down the walkway.

Once he was within five feet of the women he yelled, "Clarissa and Yasmine! What the hell is going on with you two!"

Clarissa ignored him as she continued to beat her sister relentlessly with a pole she found nearby. When Don saw an opportunity, he wrapped his chocolate muscular arms around Clarissa and used his 6'1, two-hundred-and-fifty-pound body to pick her up, moving her to the opposite side. He snatched the pole from her hands.

Tired, Clarissa bent over and placed her hands on her knees to catch her breath. Ken gave Don a signal to diffuse the altercation so the cops would not come. Out of breath, Don instructed Clarissa to go inside while he helped Yasmine.

When Ken saw that Don was taking them into the house, he rolled his eyes before speaking, "Don, make sure they are in and out because you and I need some quality time."

Don looked back giving Ken a slight smile before cutting his eyes. "Ken, don't worry, nobody is going to take your time. I got you, bae."

Inside, Clarissa kicked off her tennis shoes and began pacing the hard wood floors. Don helped Yasmine into the half bathroom. When he returned to the living room, Clarissa gestured for a cigarette. Don retrieved one for himself and tossed her the pack.

"What are you girls fighting for now?" he questioned.

Yasmine did not bother to listen to the conversation as she rested her throbbing head on the sink. The blood leaked onto the floor drip by drip from her busted nose and lip. She wished she was dead because the guilt of her failures was eating her alive. At this point, life did not mean anything. Her man Stellan constantly broke her heart; she could not shake her drug addiction, and she was a horrible mother. She did not have the courage to take her own life but hoped someone would.

In the living room, Don lit his cigarette as he listened to Clarissa explain what happened. After learning what Yasmine had done, he knew that it would only be a matter of time before Clarissa would be all over her again and he did not need any drama at home. He remembered Stellan stopping by frequently over the past week looking for Yasmine, so when Clarissa was finished, he went up to his bedroom and called him.

"Hey, Stellan, ya girl is here and not doing so well," whispered Don.

"I'm on my way," responded Stellan. He made a U-turn in his Cadillac and sped down the street.

Within five minutes, he was parking in front of Don's house. He exited the car and walked up the steep stairs. He only nodded at Ken who returned the nod before rolling the dice again. Without knocking, he opened the screen door and entered the house.

"She is in the bathroom," said Don, pointing with his cigarette.

When Stellan entered, he found Yasmine now barely able to hold herself up on the toilet. While he assessed her injuries, Yasmine mustered up the energy to speak. "Where the fuck you been?" she hissed before allowing her head to drop again.

Stellan ignored her question. Don entered the bathroom and explained everything that happened. Stellan listened without saying a word. He knew the real reason why Yasmine shot Rachel. He was having an affair with the young girl which continued when she returned to Baton City. Yasmine recently found out while going through his cell phone. It was sloppy for him to leave a trail of inboxes on social media and text messages. That night, Yasmine argued with him before leaving. The next day, when he realized she had taken his gun, he went over to her and saw the crime scene tape. For the past few weeks, he had been trying to find out exactly what happened.

When Don finished explaining, Stellan grabbed Yasmine's arm and helped her up. He put her arm over his shoulder and escorted her out the restroom.

When passing the living room, Clarissa yelled, "You are going to protect a killer!"

Stellan offered no response as he exited the front door.

Roxanne

Roxanne observed Sharae dial Zak's number. It rang several times before the voicemail picked up. Sharae sighed and left her husband an urgent message to call her back.

"Why would Kay'Ron's cousin want to harm me?" questioned Roxanne, taking a sip of her wine.

Sharae ignored her question and dialed Borya who answered on the first ring. "Hey, Borya, we figured out who attacked Roxanne. It's Carlton Reed. He is Kay'Ron's cousin on his father's side."

"Okay, send me the picture you have. Have you spoken with Zak yet?" questioned Borya.

"No, he has not answered my calls in a week, but that's nothing new," responded Sharae.

"Okay, I will try contacting him," said Borya, now looking at the photo of the man that matched the photo he already had. He ended the call and dialed Zak who did not answer his call either. He left an urgent voice message before ending the call.

WHERE IS JAY

Jay awakened from her sound sleep to people arguing in the motel room next door. Over a year ago, she traveled to Georgia to find her son Matthew. At the beginning, she spent her days searching for her son in all the obvious places. Her first stop was Donavan's house where it all started, but the place had been deserted. She found Silvia's father's address and made a trip only to find him dead in his bedroom from natural causes.

Disappointed, Jay left the house undisturbed. She knew that Donavan and Silvia had to return to Georgia for two reasons. One, they had many businesses there. Two, it was the final resting spot for Donese. At a dead end, Jay collected vital information such as birthdays, and the gravesite locations for Donese and Raymond. She faithfully visited them on birthdays and holidays in hopes of spotting Donavan and Silvia with her son. She even went as far as trying to purchase Donavan's house under a fake alias. She offered an excessive amount over market value but still no luck. Locating Donavan and his family had proven to be the hardest task she ever had on her plate.

Jay pounded her fist on the wall three times before getting out of bed. She walked over to the window, slid it open, and looked outside. She surveyed her surroundings as she did every morning. It was early but it was already a lot of activity in the parking lot.

When the tamale man Dexter noticed her, he yelled from his stand, "Hey, I will have those tamales ready for you in a few!"

Jay gave him a nod before focusing back on her arguing neighbors who were now outside. Constance threw the clothing from the balcony onto her boyfriend Jacob's car below.

"Girl, you know damn well he will be back, and you will be folding all those clothes you are throwing down there," joked Jay. They watched Jacob speed out the parking lot.

Constance turned to Jay. "He ain't shit. I am so tired of his broke ass. But I have to say you are right, he has the best dick I ever had."

They laughed. A white Bentley parked. When the driver's door opened, Zak got out. He looked up at Jay and waved before heading up the stairs.

"Damn, girl! I thought you only liked pussy," said Constance. When Zak made it upstairs, Constance's lustful stares welcomed him.

"How the fuck you find me?" questioned Jay, her voice agitated.

"Come on, baby, you know good pussy like yours can never hide! Are you going to let me in, or do I have to climb through the window for it?" joked Zak.

"Shit, you can climb through my window, I am holding the good too," interrupted Constance. She licked her lips seductively.

Zak smirked, "Don't worry, I may climb through yours next." He handed Jay the bottle of Don Julio then climbed through the window. Once inside, he continued. "So, it's like that! This is the welcome I get after not seeing you for over a year?"

Jay paced in a small area of the room as she questioned a second time how he found her.

Zak observed her open the bottle of liquor and take a gulp before he responded, "I knew you would come to Georgia first to search for Matthew, so I had my eyes on you. I like the way you're moving. The plain sight thing is smart. I wish you moved like this in the past." He looked around the room displaying a look of disgust.

"Nigga, don't act like you didn't sleep in Baton Projects with your silver spoon ass!" said Jay. They both laughed before Jay questioned, her tone now serious, "How is Priest?"

"Shit, I was hoping to find him down here with you!" responded Zak.

"Nah, he wouldn't be down here with me. Things got so bad, I thought he was going to end up snapping and killing me. He started doing drugs, displaying reckless behavior. His mood constantly shifted. He was so impulsive; I could no longer predict him."

"Damn, sis, sounds like what we were going through dealing with you."

Jay could not argue with that statement. She was the one everyone had to constantly redirect like a child. She did not realize until it was too late that everyone was just trying to help her get on the right path; from her uncle putting her into boxing to Priest trying to show her a better way.

"I should have listened to him and let him take Matthew when I got into this shit. All a nigga was trying to do is love me, now I feel like he is one of my worst enemies. I guess that's how this love shit works," said Jay, taking another drink.

Zak looked at her. It hurt him that he knew that Donavan took Matthew out of the country. He did not know exactly where but Borya informed him that Matthew was alive. Between keeping the secret of Roxanne and this, Zak was feeling like a loyal snake.

"Jay, think about this, Donavan is connected to international assassins and if they wanted Matthew dead then they would have killed him in that house. They are trying to send a different message to you. They want you to suffer. Just keep searching for your son."

Jay wanted to change the subject. "How is my bro Kay'Ron? I know losing Roxanne and both his babies has him all fucked up."

"He is coping in the worst way. Fucking everything that moves and making babies like crazy. He and Sarah have a beautiful two-year-old daughter named Eva. You know Corrine is spoiling the mess out of her. Then he has a son name Kade who's about a month old and his mother Shawneece is crazy," Zak finished.

Jay gave him a sarcastic look. "Shawneece! What's her last name? You know that nigga Marvin had a wife named Shawneece, so you better investigate that shit. By the way, what's his ass up to these days?"

"Oh, Marvin is slithering around looking for his next chance to bite. But on a better note, Natty is closer to getting released from prison. Borya has some lawyer and a close friend of Natty's that is helping her out."

"Wow, that's going to make Kay'Ron so happy. He needs his mother. I wish I had my parents," said Jay. She was feeling empty these days and wished she was surrounded by family. She knew her mother would adore Matthew while her father taught him everything he needed to know about being a man. Her brother Carter was only a baby when he died, but Jay knew he would have been the best uncle.

Zak witnessed Jay's facial expression turn from agitation to sadness. "Sis, you are not alone out here. You are my family and I love you."

"Thanks, bro, I know I always have you. I need my roll dog to go to the strip club and get up on some bitches," said Jay.

The two continued to talk and drink for the next few hours. When Dexter delivered the tamales, they ate before hitting the streets to joyride.

Mauritius Island

Donavan sat on the balcony enjoying the beautiful view of the ocean as he smoked his cigar. He loved the peace and beauty of the island, but he also missed the fast life in Atlanta. Silvia was always busy taking care of their twins, a son Dov and daughter Devora. Things were tense between them because having Matthew around reminded Donavan of how he failed his daughter. Silvia sent him to Soring Eagle but she would find out soon that was not enough.

Donavan was planning to leave for a while. He needed to get back to himself. He would miss his children when gone but he was unhappy. They found a good nanny so now was the time for him to make his move.

His thoughts were disturbed by Silvia stepping onto the balcony. "Hey, honey, I need to run some errands, the kids are playing in their room. I will be back shortly."

Her presence agitated Donavan. He gazed at the beautiful ocean view as he addressed her. "Hurry back because I have a flight to catch. I'm going to San Diego for a while to get back to some business then back to Atlanta."

Silvia clinched her teeth while griping the iron rail of the balcony. She took a deep breath. "I see you are back on this shit. You know you can handle all your business virtually." She turned to face him and pointed her finger. "I have been trying to be flexible for the past several months with your mood swings. I even sent Matthew to Soring Eagle to make you feel comfortable. You haven't had sex with me since I had the twins. Donavan, tell me, is this the end of us!" she yelled.

In an instant, Donavan was on his feet hovering over her. He responded between clinched teeth, "If you were being flexible then you would have given Matthew back to his parents and just killed Jay instead. But no, you must draw the suffering out for me. While you are looking at that little boy satisfied with revenge and showing him this fake ass love, your husband must look at him and be reminded everyday of how he failed his daughter!" He inhaled and exhaled before continuing,

"I don't need that! Give Matthew to his father and kill Jay so we can grieve the loss of my daughter and move forward. Silvia, this whole life we are living now is surrounded by what happened to Donese so how can we heal?" He went inside.

Silvia took a few minutes to process his words. She went inside with plans to continue the conversation but found him packing. "Donavan! I don't want to go back. So, what does that mean for us?"

Donavan zipped his duffle bag and tossed it by the bedroom door. "Silvia, while I am away you need to decide between your marriage or revenge on Jay. We already know where she is and can kill her. Hell, in fact, I should just go ahead and kill her so that there would be no more reasons to hide Matthew. Tell me! When will it be enough? We killed her aunt, cousin, and lover, she can't find her son. Man, she is out here bad and probably does not care if she dies at this point. If you ask me, I think we sent a damn good message, so we can move the hell on. This marriage is starting to feel like my childhood with my father. He was so stuck on revenge that he took me away from my mother, not realizing he was hurting me. Then he kills her so that we could never reunite." Tears fell from his eyes. He turned to Silvia. "I will say it one last time. Give Matthew to his father. If you decide not to, then I want a divorce."

Silvia ran across the bedroom and smacked her husband. "You have gotten so weak over the years. And these tears you are crying. I saw the weakness coming before Donese's death. That's probably why she is dead now because you're too weak to protect her."

In a rage, Donavan punched his wife, knocking her 145lb frame over the California king bed. Before she could recover from the blow, he snatched her up with one hand and pinned her against the wall. As he watched the blood stream from her nose and mouth, he spoke in a monotone voice, "You seem eager to wake a sleeping beast. Don't forget the man you married and the fact that I share blood with the person that taught you everything you know about killing." He released his grip and let her body fall to the floor.

Silvia sat on the floor wincing in pain while Donavan continued to pack. When finished, he loaded his bags into his waiting car before returning to the bedroom. Silvia was still trying to gather herself. It had been a very long time since she witnessed Donavan's wrath and the first time, he ever laid a hand on her.

"I called Dr. Martin to make a house call and our nanny will be here shortly to take care of the children while you get it together. I will check on you once I touch down in California." He left her alone in the room. Silvia had pressed him to the limit without any concern on how he was grieving their daughter's death.

In the parking lot, Kay'Ron locked his cell phone inside his glove compartment. He exited the Range Rover, then walked slowly over to the front door of the condo he purchased for Shawneece. He dreaded having to be here with her, but his son Kade needed him.

When he entered the condo, he was met by Shawneece yelling, "Where the fuck was you all day and night!"

Kay'Ron shook his head and headed back to the bedroom to check on Kade. He was still sound asleep. The poor baby had become used to his mother's yelling.

As Kay'Ron stared down at his son, he thought about ways to get them out of this toxic situation. He could always have Shawneece killed but did not want that type of Karma to fall back on him. His thoughts were interrupted by Shawneece entering the bedroom.

"We need to start working on another baby. Kade needs a little sister or brother."

Kay'Ron gave her a disgusted look. "Damn, you just pushed a baby out a month ago and you are already talking about fucking and making another one! Damn, be a woman and let your body heal." Kay'Ron shook his head and exited the bedroom, leaving Shawneece feeling stupid.

He went into the living room and sat on the couch. He was exhausted after spending all night with Sarah trying to conceive another baby. When Sarah found out about Shawneece and Kade, she insisted he give her another child. At this point, Kay'Ron needed Sarah around because he no longer had

Roxanne, so he would make her happy. He hoped she would get pregnant soon so he could stop having sex with her.

He grabbed the remote and turned to the sports channel. He watched basketball until dozing off. Soon after he was awakened by Shawneece who was on her knees. She opened his pants and wrapped her juicy lips around his semi erection. Once it was at full attention, she began sucking and slurping just the way he loved it.

Kay'Ron palmed the back of her head and began gyrating, going in and out her mouth causing her to gag. She loved it when he was ruff with her. She was so freaky, she set the bar high for the next woman. Kay'Ron knew her game, but she had no idea that sex would never keep a man for a lifetime. He released down her throat and pulled out to allow some to get on her face and freshly pressed hair. He wanted to degrade her as much as possible. Maybe if she found her self-worth, she would leave him one day.

PRIEST AND DONAVAN

At the airport, Donavan stood at the baggage carousel waiting for his luggage. He was talking with Skeet on his cell. "Brother, how are you holding up these days? I know you are carrying a lot with what happened to my niece," inquired Donavan.

"It's a lot to deal with, but she is recovering. Right now, I just need to be surrounded by family. Would you be able to come up for a couple of days? You can relax and clear your mind," said Skeet as he sat on his bedroom balcony enjoying the view of the lake.

"You know that sounds good. I have some meetings I committed to today. I will catch a flight out later tonight," responded Donavan.

"Great! Just drop your itinerary when you get things squared away. I will have a driver waiting for you," Skeet replied.

"Sounds like a plan. Oh yeah could you get some of that Baton Barbeque?" said Donavan, now grabbing his bag from the carrier.

"You got it! I heard you sent Matthew to Soring Eagle. Does this mean you voided the plan to give him back to his father?" questioned Skeet.

"The Soring Eagle was not my idea. That's Silvia and our father's bull shit. But I did not fight it. They don't understand that the kid around only reminds me of how I failed Donese. But I gave her an ultimatum: revenge, or our marriage," said Donavan.

"Damn, brother, I see you are pressing the line. But if that shit putting a strain on your marriage, then you should consider giving him back to his father yourself and moving on."

"I know I could, but honestly, it's the principle behind it. Silvia is my wife and should consider my say and feelings. She thinks I am weak and that she can disrespect me. I am a man and if she is not going to respect me and get Matthew back to his father, then I am done."

"I think she does not want to disappoint our father. You know he and Silvia have always been the same. Pops can be so extreme sometimes, especially when it comes to his family. But honestly, I don't think taking Matthew was a good move. Priest is cool and had nothing to do with the decision that Jay made," said Skeet.

"Then my intuition is right. We have been keeping this man from his son and that's why I am still suffering." Suddenly, Donavan had a feeling like someone was watching him. He turned to see a familiar face. "Hey, brother, I will text you my flight information." Donavan stared at Priest as he returned his cell to his pocket.

Both men stood toe to toe for several seconds before Priest spoke, "I am sorry about your daughter. I just want you to know that if I knew Jay was on that type of bullshit that night, I would have hogged tied her to keep her from going. I just want to know if my son is dead or alive."

Donavan felt a sense of relief hearing his words, but it would not change the fact that someone still had to pay for Donese's death. "I know you had nothing to do with it, but I need Jay to solve this," said Donavan.

"Come on, you guys killed her aunt and girlfriend, and those two people were dear to her. If Matthew is still alive, just give him back to me. He is all I have to my bloodline, I need my son," pleaded Priest.

Donavan could tell Priest truly loved Jay because even though she caused so much pain to their lives, he still tried to defend her.

"I need Jay. If you set up the kill, that will prove that you will no longer be a problem to me, and I will get your son back to you."

"You got it," said Priest, extending his hand. "I am sure she is in Georgia."

"Contact me the moment you get to her," responded Donavan, handing him a business card.

Donavan already knew where Jay was but needed to buy some time for his wife to get Matthew from Soring Eagle. The tamale man Dexter at the motel kept a close eye on Jay daily.

Priest watched Donavan walk away before reading the business card. The day had come when he had to choose between protecting Jay or saving his son. He involuntarily defended her, but in the blink of an eye, his son came first. Priest pondered in the resentment he held in his heart for Jay. At the beginning all he wanted to do was protect her and give her a better life. But Jay sabotaged herself and he could no longer be her savior. The fact that Donavan was allowing him to find Jay for him meant that Matthew was alive. His son was his legacy and if Jay had to walk the plank to save him, then Priest would deliver. He hurried to the counter and booked a one-way ticket to Georgia to find Jay.

Soring Eagle

Daubs sat inside the surveillance room observing Matthew. He was completing his 60-day physical evaluation. Matthew was making a lot of progress at school and ranked the top of his class. Daubs was now the CEO of Soring Eagle and made regular trips to the facility to check on operations and Matthew. Daubs was impressed as he watched Matthew demonstrate his martial arts skills. Suddenly, he was disturbed by one of the staff members holding the land line with a waiting call.

He took the phone knowing it could only be one of his children. When he answered hello, Silvia spoke, "Daubs, Donavan wants a divorce if I don't give Matthew back to Priest. He went back to the United States and will not return until I decide." She whispered so the nanny would not hear.

Daubs sighed before responding, "Don't worry, you just keep taking care of my grandbabies, and I will see what's going on." He ended the call.

Silvia looked at the phone, shaking her head before dialing Donavan's cell. It rang several times, but he did not answer. She didn't bother leaving a voicemail because he had not responded to the others. The thought of losing Donavan made her cry as she continued to straighten up the play area. She had underestimated how adamant he was about choosing a normal and peaceful life. She was regretting her wrath in the situation. Killing Jay or even Matthew would have made more sense in her world.

"Why did I listen to Daubs?" she questioned herself. Now that she had more children, she was content and able to move on without Matthew.

She went into her office, sat at her desk, and retrieved the contact information for Soring Eagle's enrollment department. She would disenroll Matthew, return him to his father, kill Jay, then reunite with her husband.

HOMECOMING

Borya and Abram waited at the dock as Lada steered it into the parking spot. While Borya secured the yacht, Abram helped the women step down onto the dock. Never being out of Baton City before, Rena looked around not sure where they were. In her eyes, everything looked foreign.

When Lada saw the confusion, she said, "We are in the Virgin Islands. I live here most of the year. We travel to Baton City during hurricane season." She pointed at the lavish mansion they were heading toward. Making it onto the deck, everyone stopped. Abram was strict about allowing people inside his home without proper introduction. "Rena, this is my husband Abram and son Borya." When Rena offered a smile, Lada continued. "Abram, Borya, this is Rena. I just learned that her cousin is Rachel, Skeet's daughter."

"Yes, Skeet called me and told me about his daughter. So tragic. I hate to see him suffer so much grief," said Borya.

"So, it's true? My cousin is dead?" questioned Rena.

"She will be taken off of life support in another twenty-four hours," answered Borya, his voice empathetic.

Rena began to cry. Lada wrapped her arm around her and led her inside to the family room where she took a seat on the couch. She and Borya left Abram to comfort Rena so they could discuss what was going on.

"Mom, where did you find her?" quizzed Borya.

"She was one of the prisoners in Kyle's house. The other prisoners were children, she was the oldest. She followed me to the boat and made it clear she was from the United States. While on the yacht, I noticed her eyeing Skeet's photo, so I questioned her and that's when she told me what happened. Her mother shot Rachel and Rena ran out the house to get help only to get captured and taken to Kyle's," answered Lada.

"What a traumatic day. You witness your mother shoot your cousin, you try and go for help and get abducted. Now here is where I am confused. Kyle hardly ever hunts beyond Florida,

Texas, and California because it's too risky. Why was a van in the middle of Baton City looking for girls? This looks like a planned abduction and Rena was a target but why?" pondered Borya.

"That makes sense, son. But right now, your brother needs me. His father can no longer keep me away from him," said Lada.

"We will fly out tomorrow morning at sunrise," answered Borya.

With a plan, Lada and Borya joined Abram and Rena in the kitchen. Everyone sat at the table and enjoyed a meal while conversating. For both Lada and Rena, it was ideal. Lada was able to experience the feeling of nurturing a daughter while Rena received the motherly love she never received from Yasmine.

Mexico

In Cabo, Janice walked around the rubbish of what used to be Kyle's home. She knew his death was not an accident. How did the house explode but all the children held captive survived? Before Janice could claim Kyle's body, the CIA cremated him. Janice knew it was a cover up and the answer was in Kyle's secret panic room. Only their pinky fingerprints could unlock the door to the indestructible room disguised as a massive rock alongside the mountain.

Janice made sure the coast was clear before opening the door. Once inside, she sighed in relief. It appeared nothing had been tampered with. She reviewed the footage that revealed the true story of what happened to her sacred brother. She watched Lada enter the house and kill Kyle before setting the children free.

Lada's move not only killed her brother, but it cost Janice millions of dollars because the children were hand selected and paid for by their purchasers in advance. The delivery was scheduled the day following Kyle's murder. The customers wanted their money back and Janice and Kyle had spent that money long ago.

Janice destroyed the data before exiting the panic room. She took time to take one more walk down Kyle's private beach. They were not blood, but it could not make them any closer. After her mother was murdered by Daubs, it was Kyle's family that took her in and raised her as their own.

Kyle's father, Orlando Rothers, was a high-ranking CIA Agent. He introduced his son and Janice to the world of human trafficking. Kyle followed in his father's footsteps while Janice trained to become an assassin. When Kyle's mother died of cancer, Orlando relocated his family to the Florida Keys until his untimely death years later. Kyle and Janice took over the trafficking business working with Orlando's close friend and fellow agent Rodger Locus. But when Rodger got caught up, he snitched, and Kyle had to flee to Mexico where the CIA could not touch him. This led to the CIA contracting Lada to take him out. Once he was dead, the CIA could take control over Kyle's assets and gain entry onto the property without breaking any laws in Mexico.

Janice had endured so much loss and pain from Skeet's family she could taste blood. They were the cause of her mother, brother, and Orlando's death. She had no one left to love and it was time for everyone to see her wrath. She would become a loyal snake and penetrate Skeet's circle before going in for the kill. She learned that Skeet was a man that honored truth and good deeds. The paternity results she had would prove that Rena was his daughter and that would be her trump card to get in. Nobody knew her connection to Kyle, and Daubs would not recognize her as an adult. It would be the perfect move to get revenge on Daubs and his family.

REUNITED

Today was the day that Rachel would be taken off life support. When the private jet landed, Lada, Rena, and Borya exited. They wasted no time getting inside the SUV that was waiting to take them to the hospital. After an evening of Clarissa and her family gathering at Rachel's bedside to say their final goodbyes, Skeet instructed the hospital to not allow anyone else to see his daughter.

As Rena road, she could not hold back tears. Visions of her mother shooting Rachel ran marathons in her head. It began to rain, making things more depressing. Lada placed her hand on Rena's in attempts to console her.

Once Rachel was gone, she would have no one. She hated her mother and would never allow her in her life again. Her other family were hardly around so they did not matter. When they arrived at the main entrance of the hospital, everyone got out and hurried inside.

The elevator ride to the seventh floor seemed to take an eternity. When they exited the elevator, Skeet was waiting in the hall for them. When he laid eyes on Rena, the shock was evident in his face.

Borya spoke, "Hey, brother I will explain everything. In fact, let's just start with me introducing you to our mother."

Borya turned, using his arms in a dramatic way. He presented Lada who was standing slightly behind him. She removed her black hood allowing him to see her face.

Overwhelmed with emotions, Skeet opened his arms as he approached her. He had to bend down slightly to meet her 5'1 height for a hug. They embraced for several minutes. Borya took the liberty of taking Rena to see Rachel so that Skeet and Lada could have their moment.

Before going into the door, Rena stopped to gather herself.

"Take all the time you need. I understand your pain," said Borya.

She took a deep breath and entered the room. The sight of her in the bed flooded Rena with emotions all over again. Rachel was hooked up to several life sustaining machines. The respirator manipulating her chest to rise and fall made Rena feel sick to her stomach. Her face was pale. When Rena touched her arm, it felt cold and clammy. Rena spoke softly, "I am so sorry, Rachel. I don't know why my mother did this to you. We have been through so much, you can't leave me like this, you are the only family I have now." She sat on the chair alongside the bed and laid her head on it before closing her eyes.

Trauma was all the girls experienced while growing up and Rachel had endured the most. It was just the two of them for several years before Clarissa gave birth to Ebony. The girls witnessed drug dealing, fatal shootouts, drug addicts, and bloody fights between their mother's and other family members. The only consistent people they had to take care of them were their grandparents Eula and Joe, but they were now too elderly and sick to keep up with the girls.

The worse experience was when Rachel was raped by their Aunt Linda's ex-husband Warren. Eula was the one that entrusted him with the girls after he made a good impression. He earned his keep through helping around the house. Eula was blinded and felt he was the best son-in-law. She didn't understand why her daughter had divorced him.

Instead of warning her family about Warren, Linda dropped all seven of her children to their father once the money ran out. She knew that Warren was molesting her daughters, but the money kept her quiet. When Warren went broke, Linda planned to get out and leave the country. Her children were happy to get out of the situation and agreed to never speak of it to their biological father. The silence left Warren a free man to prey on another little girl.

One Saturday morning, everyone decided to go and help Joe with the family business of cleaning a local building. Rena and Rachel were asleep on the third floor in separate rooms. When everyone was gone, Warren crept up the narrow stairs. He checked to make sure Rena was asleep before going into Rachel's bedroom.

Rena was awakened by the screams from the next room. She slid out of bed and headed to Rachel's room only to stand in front of a locked door. Rena could do nothing but wait. A half hour later, Warren opened the door and came out carrying Rachel. He walked past Rena as if she was not there and went downstairs to the second floor. Rena followed behind them worried and confused about what was happening. Warren entered the restroom and placed Rachel inside the tub. He cleaned her up and returned her to bed. Next, he took Rena downstairs to the kitchen and fixed her a bowl of cereal before retreating to his bedroom. He got high and fell into a deep sleep.

Rena sat at the kitchen table alone, afraid to move from her seat. She looked at the front door hoping that someone would come home. A couple of hours later, everyone came in the door. When Lloyd entered the kitchen, he looked at his niece and knew something was wrong. He leaned down in front of her and asked what was wrong. Rena, who was four years old, did not know how to explain what she witnessed so she just pointed upward.

"Show me," said Lloyd as he took Rena's hand helping her from the chair.

He alerted everyone and they followed. On the second floor, Lloyd noticed drops of blood. He looked back at his mother and brother Anthony. They followed the trail to the restroom.

"Who was in the tub, Rena?" questioned Lloyd, thinking that it was probably Yasmine's blood from one of her street battles.

Rena uttered, "Rachel and Warren."

Eula put her right hand on her chest and headed to the third set of stairs leading to the third floor. Lloyd and Anthony went into Warren's bedroom.

Rena stood in the middle of the hall not knowing if she should have followed Eula or her uncles. When Anthony and Lloyd entered the room, Warren was asleep snoring with the needle still lodged in his arm. Lloyd pointed at the blood on his zipper and started to lunge for Warren, but Anthony pulled him back out of the bedroom.

"Let's make this count," he whispered to his older brother.

Anthony hurried to Rachel's bedroom and took her from her bed, downstairs to the living room with everyone else.

Hours later, everyone was home and informed of what happened to Rachel. Despite all the drama, drugs, and dysfunction between the siblings, Rachel and Rena took precedence. Clarissa contacted Skeet. He sent one of his doctor friends over to check on Rachel. When the doctor examined her, Rena observed her uncles in the dining room loading a gun and untangling rope.

This day was the only time Yasmine was very tentative to her daughter. The family made a pact that the events that would take place that night would never be shared with anyone who was not present. When Skeet arrived, he backed the old rusted burgundy van up the long narrow driveway that wrapped to the back of the house. He hopped out and grabbed the body bag he picked up from his father's funeral home. When he entered through the backdoor, all the men sat in the kitchen.

Upstairs, Warren continued to sleep, unaware there was any danger. When he finally awakened, he got up and took the needle out of his arm. He put on a tank top and walked out of his room. When he came around the corner, he was intercepted by Anthony. He knocked him out and dragged his limp body back into the bedroom. While unconscious, the men tied Warren to a chair before waking him. For several hours, Joe, Anthony, and Skeet beat him relentlessly while Lloyd burned him with cigarettes. Then Skeet pistol whipped him before screwing on his silencer and emptying the clip into Warren.

Afterwards, they placed his body in the body bag. Anthony and Skeet tossed him in the back of the van and went to Skeet's father's crematory. Lloyd and Joe stayed behind cleaning up and disposing of any evidence. No one would ever find Warren.

NEW BEGINNINGS

Karen opened the door to one of the lofts in Kay'Ron's building. "I hope you find this place suitable to fit your needs."

Rena walked in slowly taking in the place, she could already visualize how she would decorate.

Seconds later, Borya walked in and greeted everyone. "What do you think? A place to call your own," questioned Borya.

"Wow, this place is amazing. But I know I can't afford it," answered Rena.

"Don't worry, my mother will be paying for everything. All you need to do is follow your dreams and don't do anything stupid," replied Borya.

"What! This is a dream come true. Lada has nothing to worry about. I am forever in her debt for this," said Rena, admiring the view of the downtown area.

"No worries, you just need to use this as an opportunity to start a new life. Lada has a boutique two doors down that you will oversee. You start tomorrow morning at 9:00am sharp," said Borya, tossing Rena a set of keys.

Rena examined the keys noticing there was a car key attached. "Borya, I think you gave me too many keys," she spoke, attempting to hand them back, but Borya stopped her.

"No, you have a car as well, happy eighteenth birthday! Skeet told us your birthday was tomorrow. And you need a car to go shopping to find furniture, groceries, household supplies, and clothing for your new job." Borya handed her a credit card and an envelope full of cash.

Rena was speechless. It was like life was finally in her favor. However, it saddened her that it was at the cost of her cousin's life. If her mother had not shot Rachel, then Rena would never have run out of the house which meant she would not have been abducted. It's ironic how bad situations happen only to lead you to something greater.

"I know some good places to shop, I don't mind showing you around," said Karen.

"Well, I will leave you ladies to it. Your car is parked in your private parking spot out back," said Borya before leaving.

Once he was gone Karen spoke, "Damn, girl! I never had anyone come through for me like this. Honey, you are truly blessed."

"Yes, I am. It's like my life was fucked up, then the door just opened and now things are great," responded Rena.

"Well, it's two o'clock so you don't have much time. Let's go, I will take you to get your essentials. You don't want to rush and buy any type of furniture, so let's get you a good quality airbed, a couple bar stools, personal and household items, and a few outfits to get you through the week. We can do your grocery order online while we enjoy a late dinner at Natty's in a few hours. The grocery store in the neighborhood delivers groceries until midnight," suggested Karen.

"Okay, well, let's find this new car I have," said Rena, looking out the back window at the cars in the parking lot. She pressed the key fob and the lights blinked on a white BMW.

"Well, damn, girl, that is the newest BMW, so I know it's fully loaded." The girls laughed, exiting the back door. They playfully raced each other to the car.

At Skeets mansion, everyone gathered in the family room awaiting dinner prepared by Lada.

"Brother, your mother in the kitchen preparing a meal is a blessing. I wish I could remember my mother's cooking," said Donavan before taking a drink.

"Just consider my mother yours. I know it must be hard loving the man that is responsible for your mother's death," responded Skeet.

"I remember how he would never allow us to even say the word mother," Donavan stated.

"You think I took your mother because of pain?" asked Daubs, entering the family room. He poured himself a drink. He then took a seat across from his sons. "Let's continue this conversation. I gave both of you the best life without a mother. I made hard decisions to protect you two and placed my feelings to the side. Since we are speaking our minds, Skeet, you should have made the decision a long time ago to not give a damn about Clarissa's say and take your daughter. Now she's upstairs in a coma and you are planning a botch funeral. And, Donavan, your wife avenged your daughter's death, and you threaten to divorce her. I am disappointed."

His words stung but only Donavan showed it. Skeet was tougher because he had been through a lot with his father and there was always the day he dreamed of reuniting with his mother. But Donavan would always have a void in his heart because his mother was taken away from him at the hands of his father. He had to learn to love the person that caused him the most pain. For years, his father's influence got him through the bad days when he missed his mother. But when he found out his younger brother Larry died, he had been grieving the loss of both and the days were not getting easier.

Daubs killing his mother also only sent the message that a family could be discarded. Unlike Skeet, whose parents were both killers, Donavan's mother was just a regular person living life in the world instead of above it. He was old enough to witness some of her struggles, especially after she tried to move on from his father. He remembered Daubs coming to their apartment and taking him away from his mother. He would never forget his mother chasing the car down the block.

Donavan knew his mother loved him. He truly believed he possessed a lot of her ways. She was a loving human; his father was an inhumane beast. Donavan's DNA was filled with love and humanity while his environment created the beast that he tried to keep locked within.

After Daubs statement, neither Skeet nor Donavan bothered to say anything. They were used to their father's harshness, and it was no point in arguing because he felt he knew everything.

"You are right, dad, I should have taken Rachel a long time ago," said Skeet, going to the bar to fix him another drink.

"What about you Donavan?" questioned Daubs.

"You're always right, father, I have no input," responded Donavan.

Satisfied, Daubs went to the kitchen. When he entered, Lada was standing in the middle of the floor with her hands on her hips. She had overheard all the conversation and was disappointed that Daubs stripped them away from their mother's, only to make them victims of his manipulation.

"So, this is the bull you have been doing to these boys all their lives?" questioned Lada, her voice callous.

Daubs smirked, taking a seat on one of the barstools. Lada was one of the three women in his life that could call him out on his shit without losing their life behind it.

"What can I say, Lada, I am raising men over here. We both know this world is not for the weak, so why torment ourselves with the agony of watching our off springs be consumed by the world." He took a drink. "These so-called men have allowed bad things to happen to our precious legacies. Now I have a dead granddaughter and another upstairs in a coma."

"Maybe if they would have been nurtured by their mother's, they would have an understanding on how to protect the women in their family because they would be doing it from the heart and not for control," countered Lada.

"Lada, you know that is bullshit. Nurturing creates a window for weakness. What I despise about this world is that everyone wants the benefits without doing any hard work."

"Hard work! Based on what I have heard these men speak about, they were not allotted a normal childhood. They had to do a lot of hard work for a man that took their mothers away," argued Lada.

"I will say it again. I raised them to be strong in this world. Remember, we did not want them to suffer like we did as children. Making them strong comes at a cost. I was born into trauma; you were born into both poverty and trauma. We both survived some horrific things. You witnessed your parents' murder. I found my father hanging after he murdered the only two people that loved me. Crying was a luxury and made no sense in our lives," countered Daubs.

"You are right, we can't all have balance, but we need some type of love for humanity. Yes, it comes with its weaknesses but what is the point of creating a life if you can't have love and connection? I am sure at this point you have successfully instilled the beast you wanted into your boys, but now allow me to give them a softer side," finished Lada. She turned and continued stirring the oxtails on the stove.

Daubs sat quietly thinking as he observed Lada in the kitchen. He had never seen her in this form because their lives together were filled with disparity. They connected as prisoners and fell for each other during grave circumstances. They used their power to fight together and created a life that represented their love. Lada held one of the keys to his heart, but it was Daubs stubbornness that would not allow them to ever be. So, she moved on and found the love he could not give. He understood his errors but the path he chose in this world meant there had to be a sacrifice and that was his heart.

Not wanting to dwell in his feelings he changed the subject. "On another note, great work on that Kyle situation."

"Yeah, I basically finished what you and my son started. Tell me, why you didn't just kill him?" said Lada, placing a plate of oxtails and rice in front of him.

"Shit, he raped Sanity, he was not going to get the easy way out. It was our lovely son's idea to castrate him and make him suffer," responded Daubs, grabbing his fork.

Lada watched him bite into one of the oxtails. He took a moment to savor the flavor before taking another bite. "I get it, you wanted him to suffer. But then many children suffered including Rachel's cousin Rena who was being held captive. Just think if it was Rachel running out that night; they would have gotten her instead. I believe she was really the target because she is Skeet's daughter."

"Nah, Kyle does not miss his target. The question is what makes Rena significant enough to capture instead of Rachel? They could have just done a home invasion and got her. How were they able to be precise enough to catch that girl during that time? Yeah, they could have been staking out and saw the commotion. But knowing Rachel was injured, it would have made sense to just abort the mission," answered Daubs.

"Has anyone found Yasmine yet?" questioned Lada.

"Yes, Skeet has that covered. He will handle it before the graveside service in a couple days," responded Daubs, focusing back on his food.

Satisfied, Lada did not respond. She turned around and continued preparing the meal. When finished, she prepared the dining table. When it was time for everyone to sit and eat, Daubs was long gone. However, no one was surprised because he rarely did the family thing.

THE BEGINNING OF THE END

Rena hung the lunch sign in the window before closing and locking the door to the boutique. She walked two doors down to Natty's where Karen was waiting for her. While walking, her phone began to vibrate. She read the text message from Borya; he checked on her daily. Not paying attention, she bumped into someone.

"Oh, shit my bad," Rena spoke, looking up.

Kay'Ron hovered over her offering a charming smile. Rena returned the smile and proceeded to the front door of Natty's. Before she could touch the handle, Kay'Ron opened it and gestured for her to go inside.

"Umm, thank you," said Rena before going in. She found Karen sitting at one of the tables drinking a margarita. Rena hurried over and took a seat. "Girl, who is that man? He is so fine." Questioned Rena.

Karen frowned before responding, "Who Kay'Ron? Yeah, he is fine but girl he is a handful. He is quite the charmer, so if you fall into his web, just watch yourself. He has a lot going on."

Rena turned around and looked at Kay'Ron. He was now behind the bar talking with one of the employees.

"He works here?" she questioned.

"He is the owner of this establishment and the place you live," said Karen, waving the waiter over. The girls ordered their lunch before continuing their conversation. "I can see now that you are going to probably let him get it if he pursues you, so I will give you the low down."

"Let him get what?" questioned Rena.

"Girl the pussy!" said Karen, letting out a giggle.

Rena did not laugh because she was still a virgin. When Karen stopped laughing and looked at Rena's concerned expression, she placed her hand on her chest. "OMG! You are a virgin. Damn, I have never seen one over the age sixteen before. These days they want to hurry up and give it away like it's a virus," joked Karen.

Embarrassed, Rena spoke defensively, "Yes, I am, I did not get out much." She knew her answer was stupid, but she had to respond.

"Don't worry, girl! It's nothing to be ashamed of. It's rare. I wish I had mines because I have given it to so many men, I regret. If I could start all over, I would only give myself to Zak." Karen stared off into space. She had been in a complicated relationship with Zak for a few years.

He did just enough to keep her satisfied as his trap house wifey. When Zak was in town, they spent a lot of time together. But Karen was falling in love with him and wanted more. Zak was into her also, but nothing would make him divorce Sharae. Karen knew about his wife and children and Zak knew that one day she would get tired of being his side chick. Until then, he would play on Karen's adverse circumstances.

When their food was ready, Kay'Ron put on an apron. He grabbed the plates and headed over to their table.

"Okay, I have crabcakes for you, beautiful. I already know the fried chicken strips with honey mustard sauce belongs to Karen," said Kay'Ron with a smirk.

Karen playfully rolled her eyes before digging into her food. Rena took a bite of one of the crabcakes and savored the flavor.

Kay'Ron stood patiently until she finished chewing. "I see you like the crabcakes. You should come back later, it's seafood night. I can reserve us a private booth."

Karen stayed focused on her plate, allowing Rena to make the decision on whether she wanted to go there. The selfish side of her thought it would be good for them to be with cousins so they could spend more time with each other. However, she knew Kay'Ron's track record and would dread wiping Rena's tears later.

Rena took the bait, agreeing to have dinner with Kay'Ron. Satisfied, he left them to finish their lunch and when it was time to pay the bill, the girls learned that everything was on the house.

"Well, damn, I need to eat lunch with you more often! Kay'Ron doesn't even allow his employees to eat for free," joked Karen.

Rena laughed, standing up from her chair. Kay'Ron watched her straighten out her blue floral mini dress. The dress was not form fitting, but he could tell she had a nice ass. Her skin was the perfect cocoa complexion, and her natural unmade up beauty was complimented by long natural sandy brown hair that reached her midback. She seemed to trigger the same arousal out of him like Roxanne once did.

He could tell that Rena was nothing like women he was currently dealing with. Like Sarah and Shawneece, they spent hours in the bathroom making up their faces. He hated makeup and found it humorous when women could not cry properly because they were so concerned with their makeup. If you can't even do natural things like walk in the rain or cry freely, then what was the point. Rena was the type of girl he could take to his new lake house and skinny dip with her without her worrying about her wig, weave, glue, or makeup. He imagined gripping a handful of her thick hair and tasting every part of her. He was so wrapped up in his imagination he didn't realize that Rena was gone.

He went over to Karen as she was finishing up her food. "I did not know you had a best friend because you are always under my cousin," he spoke in a sarcastic voice.

Karen took her time using the toothpick to get some chicken out of her teeth before responding, "Kay'Ron, don't play with my friend. She just turned eighteen and she is still…" Karen stopped, almost revealing to Kay'Ron that Rena was a virgin.

But he was no fool, the only other thing that could have come after those words would be 'with another nigga' and in Kay'Ron's world, niggas never got in his way and Karen knew that. The thought of Rena never being with anyone made him want her more.

"Don't worry, your friend is in good hands," said Kay'Ron, walking away.

Despite his messy love life, he could not let Rena pass him by. He found it ironic that he was imagining longevity with a woman he did not know. Is this what it meant when people spoke of love at first sight? He already felt protective of her and wanted to handle her with care instead of fucking and leaving her. Her natural scent still lingered in his nostrils. He was literally like a dog in heat and could sniff her out anywhere. He had to have her.

Now back at the boutique, Rena put her purse up before joining Lada at the counter to square the books. "Rena, you are getting the hang of things. It has not been a full month and I seem to never have to come to check on things," said Lada.

"Thank you, I never thought I would be doing this. I really appreciate all you have done for me," responded Rena.

"Any family of Rachel is my family," replied Lada.

Mentioning Rachel made Rena feel sad. Her funeral service was the following day. Lada could see her mood dampened so she changed the subject. "I saw that handsome guy hovering over you in front of Natty's."

"Lada, he is so fine, I can't believe he asked me to dinner later! It's seafood night at Natty's."

"Very good. Well, you enjoy, there is nothing wrong with a man wining and dining you. Make him roll out the biggest red carpet because you are special."

"I will, this would be my first date," said Rena.

Lada went over to one of the dresses in the window. It was a pink satin mini dress with spaghetti strings that would complement Rena's perfect shoulders and toned legs. She took the dress off the mannequin and gave it to Rena. "This here will have him dreaming about you every night. The perfect dress to validate you are a woman. Strut and show your power but be careful. Be ready for anything and if he gets disrespectful, kick him in the balls, then call me or Borya."

Rena nodded before heading back into the dressing room to try on the dress. As she slipped it on, the pink satin material slid over her skin so soft, she felt a tingle between her legs. The dress made her feel sexy. When she looked in the mirror, the vision made her want to fuck her damn self. This dress was perfect, like it was made just for her.

Rena walked out of the dressing room. Lada placed her hands over her mouth amazed at how she looked. "It's simple, just right for you! A small tote and bracelet. Wear your hair down. He is going to eat you alive my dear," said Lada. She selected a pink satin tote and a simple diamond bracelet and handed it over to Rena. "You're all set."

THE HUNT

Across town, Skeet sat down the street waiting for Yasmine to come out of Don's house. He watched the sunset as he thought about how he would finally get revenge for his daughter. An hour later, Yasmine exited the house. She had been awake for two days straight drinking and drugging to face the next day. Before leaving Don's, she made the decision to take responsibility for her actions. She would go to her niece's funeral to apologize to everyone and say goodbye to Rachel. She counted on the authorities apprehending her at the services.

While Don and Ken were in the bedroom, Yasmine exited the house and staggered down the walkway, not paying attention to her surroundings. It was summertime but today no one was hanging out like usual because they were at the annual Baton City festival.

Like a thief in the night, Skeet crept from the shadows of the darkness. He used his extensive marine training to apprehend Yasmine. With one move, she was puddy in his arms. A black van with tinted windows pulled up and the side door slid open. Skeet tossed her inside like a rag doll before getting in. As Tobias drove, Skeet continuously beat Yasmine. Thirty minutes later, they arrived at the cemetery. He exited the van and pulled Yasmine out of it, dragging her to the freshly dug grave.

"Time to pay for what you did to my daughter," spoke Skeet. When they made it to the open grave, he kicked her inside. Realizing she was being buried alive, Yasmine began to panic. Skeet smirked while speaking, "Don't be afraid now, you knew the moment you shot my daughter I would come for you."

Yasmine spit blood from her mouth. "I should have sold her like I did Rena instead."

"And we would have found her like we did Rena. Your daughter is back here living her best life forgetting about you," spat Skeet. He grabbed the shovel and began tossing dirt onto Yasmine.

Desperate, she began taunting him in hopes he would put a bullet into her head and end things quick, "Some father you are, leaving your daughter in the hands of junkies while you traveled the world and made money. You want to know what your precious Rachel did to me? She was fucking my man behind my back. That bitch was thirsty for my man's dick!" Yasmine yelled.

"Oh really, who Stellan? Good to know there is someone else I need to handle," responded Skeet.

"You know what, you can kill me, but I will still get the last laugh!" shrieked Yasmine.

Ready to go, Skeet instructed Tobias to push the empty casket inside the grave insuring that Yasmine would not climb her way out. He was sure the impact of the casket would severely injure or kill her. He climbed inside the bobcat, turned it on, and pushed the mountain of dirt, filling the grave. When finished, he sat a red rose in the middle of the pile of unsettled dirt. "Goodbye, Yasmine."

At Natty's, Kay'Ron sat at the bar waiting patiently for Rena to arrive. He had selected a private room for dining in the back of Natty's in the VIP section. He was excited because he had not had a romantic night since Roxanne.

In the loft next door, Karen stood watching Rena admiring herself in the mirror. "Girl, you are going to lose that virginity tonight," said Karen.

It wasn't the goal to do this, but Rena was feeling an energy she had never felt before. The dress seemed to ignite her root chakra and she was down for whatever happened. She needed a night to forget about everything and enjoy happy things because the following day she would be laying her cousin Rachel to rest.

"Okay, I am ready for this seafood," said Rena, heading to the door to leave.

"Uh yeah and Kay'Ron is ready to make you his food," joked Karen. The ladies laughed as they rode down the elevator. When they exited, Karen walked Rena to the main entrance.

"Hey, young lady, you take care of yourself. Kay'Ron is going to treat you right but don't do anything you don't want to do."

"Don't worry, Karen, I got this. Will you be here when I get back?" queried Rena.

"Hell no! Girl, you are kicking it with Kay'Ron tonight. Please believe that damn seafood is not all he has in store for you. Let's just say you're not going to bed until sunrise and that does not necessary mean you two will be up fucking. I just know him and his cousin are fun. They live it up and money is never a thing with them," answered Karen.

Rena smiled and exited the building. She did not have to worry about the hot July summer heat making her sweat now that the sun had set. She took in the fresh air before walking next door to Natty's. When she entered, Kay'Ron hurried over to greet her. He was impressed that she was on time and did not keep him waiting. He took her in from head to toe. He admired her attire; she made something simple look sexy as fuck and he loved that.

"You look beautiful," he stated, taking her hand and guiding her to the private room.

When Rena entered, she inspected the décor. The walls were painted black. Intimate paintings hung on the wall of naked men and women in various poses. There was a water fountain in the corner of the room shaped as a naked woman looking up to the sky. Rena followed the trail of white roses to the table. Kay'Ron pulled her seat out to sit before he took his seat across from her. Rena observed the different bottles of wine on the table. She had never had wine before but always wondered what it was like to drink a glass like the women in the movies.

Moments later, the waiter walked in with a large platter containing shrimp, lobster, king crab legs, chilled oysters, and squid. Another waiter entered with a tray containing two plates of New York strip steaks medium well and side salads.

Rena took a drink of her glass of water as she decided what she wanted to eat first. Everything was like a movie, even the handsome man that sat across from her.

"I hope you like your steak medium well," said Kay'Ron, cutting his steak. He forked a piece of his meat and reached across the table. "The chef makes his steaks almost better than me."

Rena ate the meat off the fork and savored the tenderness and flavor. "Damn, you said you can make a steak better than that?"

"Don't worry, you will find out soon," answered Kay'Ron before digging into his food.

They ate for several minutes in silence. Rena didn't care about talking because the food was so good. She was ashamed to admit this was her first-time eating steak; that was considered a luxury in her household. The only time she ate seafood was when she was with her aunt Clarissa.

Kay'Ron opened a couple bottles of wine. He chose a cabernet and sweet red. "Okay, when it comes to wine drinking, you have to decide if you like sweet or dry," Kay'Ron spoke as he poured a small amount of each wine in separate glasses.

Rena tasted the sweet red and nodded in approval. Kay'Ron encouraged her to try the dry and when she did, she approved of that as well. "Oh, I see you on your grown woman shit liking that dry wine. Personally, I think it's a classier choice," said Kay'Ron, pouring himself a glass of cabernet. "Are you from Baton City? Karen told me you lived in one of my lofts next door."

"Yep, born and raised here, my family was complicated. We didn't have money," replied Rena before eating the shrimp.

"Well, looks like you are doing well for yourself, you paid up for a year."

"It's a long story," responded Rena before taking another drink of her wine.

Kay'Ron topped her glass. "Well, we have time."

For the next few hours, Rena explained to Kay'Ron how she was abducted and held captive before meeting Lada. As Kay'Ron listened, he could not help but think about how Borya was involved in every situation around him. He had helped Roxanne obtain two high-end properties and now he conducted a lot of business with his cousin Zak. His hood nigga mindset screamed Feds but there were no crimes being committed to obtain the wealth he had gained. Natty's and the lofts paid for themselves. All he had to do was keep the tenants and customers happy.

When it got late, Kay'Ron and Rena went over to Rena's place where they continued the night drinking wine and conversating. They drank so much they ended up falling asleep on the living room floor. The next morning when Rena awakened, Kay'Ron was gone. When she checked her phone, he texted her inviting her to come over for breakfast when she awakened. Hungry, Rena showered, dressed, and went over to Natty's. Kay'Ron was sitting at one of the tables talking with an employee. When he saw Rena, he came to her and took her over to one of the booths by the window.

"Order whatever you want, I will be right over after I wrap this meeting up," said Kay'Ron before returning to the table.

While reviewing the menu, one of the waiters came over with a complementary mimosa. When Rena looked over at Kay'Ron, he winked. She smiled and thanked him. She ordered T-bone steak, sunny side up eggs, and hashbrowns along with another mimosa. The day was starting off well, but Rachel's graveside service was scheduled for late afternoon. Rena gazed out the window thinking about her cousin. She still could not believe she was dead.

Moments later, Karen called. She answered. "Girl! You were supposed to call me as soon as you opened your eyes or was you riding dick?" said Karen, relaxing on the couch.

Rena laughed, "I was invited to breakfast, and I am still a virgin."

"Wait, what? Kay'Ron wined and dined you and y'all did not fuck?" said Karen, now sitting on the edge of the couch.

"No, we fell asleep and when I awakened, he texted me to come over for breakfast," answered Rena, looking over at Kay'Ron. He appeared to be finishing up his meeting.

"Oh shit, honey, you have to be something special because I have never heard of Kay'Ron not getting in the panties the first night."

Karen's words made Rena think. Was Kay'Ron really trying to get to know her. He never made any sexual advances towards her even after they were tipsy. When Kay'Ron was heading over, she ended the call with Karen.

"Tell Karen you good," joked Kay'Ron, taking a seat across the table. Rena giggled and took a sip of her mimosa. "The boutique is not open today?"

"No, I will be attending a funeral late afternoon. It's my cousin Rachel," answered Rena.

"Oh wow, my condolences, losing a loved one is never easy," said Kay'Ron.

"Thank you for kind words. This is all a lot for me, but I am looking forward to a new beginning," answered Rena.

"New beginning, I like that," retorted Kay'Ron.

When the food arrived, Rena ate while Kay'Ron kept the mimosa's coming. When Rena was finished eating, he walked her over to her place. Rena was tipsy as she held on to his strong arm. When they made it to her place, they went inside where Rena plopped down on the couch.

"What time do you need to be ready for the funeral?" questioned Kay'Ron.

"3:00 this afternoon. Never been to a funeral so late in my life. And it's at the cemetery, that's so weird to me," answered Rena, kicking off her shoes.

Kay'Ron checked his watch, it was 11:30am. He went to the kitchen and looked in the fridge to find a bottle of water. He brought it to Rena and instructed her to drink it as he went into her bathroom to find aspirin in the medicine cabinet. When he returned, Rena was lying on the couch.

"We need to get you right for the funeral service," said Kay'Ron, taking a seat on the couch. He put her legs on his lap and sat quietly while Rena lay with her eyes closed. She took for granted the power of champagne and orange juice.

"I am definitely not messing with anything sweet moving forward," she spoke never opening her eyes.

Kay'Ron laughed. "I should have stopped you when you were on your fourth one."

"Yeah, you should have," said Rena.

"I know a way to sober you up enough to function," suggested Kay'Ron. Rena opened one eye looking at him waiting for an answer. "I think I should just show you instead of explaining."

"I am down for anything that will get me to that funeral."

Kay'Ron moved Rena's legs from his lap and stood over her holding his hand. "Trust me," he stated.

Rena took his hand and allowed him to guide her to the bedroom. Once inside, Kay'Ron guided her to the bed. He kissed her lips gently and laid her down before slipping her shorts off. Rena laid in silence, her heart pounding. This was the moment she was waiting for, but she was nervous.

"Don't worry, I know you've never done this before," whispered Kay'Ron.

He planted his face between her legs. He swirled his tongue around her clitoris gently, savoring her sweetness. Rena had never felt anything this good before. She released low wining moans of pleasure as Kay'Ron continued tasting her. Her moans aroused him more causing him to flick his tongue faster. He ravished her delicate flesh. Rena writhed all over the bed in pure ecstasy as her juices poured from her core. All these feelings surged through her body, she thought she would explode. Her body began shaking uncontrollably and she released a wining moan as she climaxed.

Kay'Ron ejaculated in his pants, and it was the most invigorating feeling he had ever felt without penetration. He lifted his head from between Rena's legs and looked at her. "How you feel now?" he questioned, standing to his feet.

Rena took a moment to gather herself. "I feel like I'm floating on air."

Satisfied, Kay'Ron smiled. "Well, at least you're relaxed and not tipsy anymore. You should be good for later. When you have time, hit me up. Maybe we can do late dinner or breakfast again. I promise I will cook in your kitchen this time."

Not bothering to wait for her response, he exited the room confident that she would contact him soon.

GOODBYE YASMINE

"We gather here to say goodbye to our beloved Rachel. The family has requested that we keep it short. So, Lord, speak through me today so that I can pour comfort and strength into this family during these trying times," spoke the pastor.

Everyone gathered for the graveside service to say goodbye to the person who they thought was Rachel. This would be the first time Rena would see her family and she was not sure how they would react. Over the past month, she checked the websites and called the police department to see if she was reported missing. But there was nothing.

Arriving early, she took a seat in the last row of chairs. In efforts to conceal herself, she wore a pair of Gucci sunglasses and a big black straw hat. But her efforts had failed when her aunt Clarissa arrived. She instantly noticed her niece and confronted her, "Where have you been, Rena? Why were you not there to help my daughter!"

"I tried to go for help but—"

Rena was cut off by Clarissa, "I ran into your mother and beat the hell out of her. I wish I would have killed her."

"I wish you would have killed her too," said Rena.

Clarissa was surprised to hear the words from her niece's mouth. She looked at her from head to toe before speaking, "Rena, you look expensive. Where have you been hiding these past few weeks?"

Before Rena could respond, Lada intervened, "I have been looking out for the young lady since her family seemed to have abandoned her." Clarissa turned her nose up and walked away. Lada took a seat next to Rena and put her arm around her offering her comfort. "Don't worry, we are your family now and we have your back."

Suddenly, there was a commotion going on at the front row. "Skeet, you son of a bitch! What type of service is this! I wanted a viewing!" yelled Clarissa.

She dropped to her knees on the freshly covered grave with a massive headstone that read 'Jones'. Skeet went over to her, kneeled by her side, then wrapped his arms around her, appearing to be comforting her. He whispered in her ear, "Bitch, if you don't get your shit together you are going to be lying next to her. I have allowed you to control our daughter all these years and now it's my turn." He stood up and helped Clarissa from the ground before guiding her to her seat.

As the service proceeded, Clarissa gave both Rena and Skeet dirty looks. Skeet kept his cool because he had nothing to be sad about. Early that morning, Rachel had awakened from her coma. She lost her memory, but the doctor advised it could be temporary but only time would tell. For Skeet, it was like a second chance. He would spend his time creating memories with his daughter and when or if she regained her memory, he would deal with that.

Not wanting to stay any longer, Rena went to her car. Lada observed her driving away before looking over at Skeet who also noticed. Now that they were sure she wanted nothing to do with her family, they planned to tell her that Rachel was alive.

"Ashes to ashes, dust to dust. The Daubs and Jones family thank everyone for their love and support during this trying time. The Jones family will be hosting a repast celebration at the Baton City Community Center. The address is on the back of the program," the Paster concluded.

Clarissa lunged out of her seat and tossed her body onto the grave and began crying was she yelled, "Why lord! What will I do without her!"

Various family and friends ran to her aid. Skeet stood up and walked away, finding shade under a tree nearby and gaining distance between him and the crowd. He took out his cigar, lit it, and began taking puffs while watching the show.

A woman approached him from behind. "Excuse me, sir," said Janice.

Skeet turned in agitation expecting to find one of Clarissa's relatives. But when he laid eyes on Janice, she was a cool breeze in the smoldering heat. Her tall, slim frame reminded him of the perfect model but slightly thicker. Her bronze skin was smooth like silk. Her DD breasts wanted to burst out of her sleeveless top. Her hazel green eyes illuminated her beautiful face complimenting her full lips. Skeet lusted over her for several seconds, he hoped she was a groupie coming to console him because he planned to take full advantage.

Janice allowed him to lust over her a bit longer. She knew that a woman's power was her sexy and she would use any and everything to get Skeet where she wanted him. To ensure that she kept his attention, she would reveal the critical information she possessed.

"I have some very important information for you," said Janice, revealing a brown envelope. Handing it over to Skeet, she continued, "Yasmine was keeping a secret from you. Rena is your daughter, and the results are in that envelope."

Skeet looked at the envelope, his lustful stare now confused and callous. What type of content could be in the envelope that would prove Rena was his daughter.

Janice read his expression and continued, "When you were incarcerated and your DNA was collected, Yasmine gave birth to Rena and requested a DNA test. Since you were an inmate, the state did not need your consent. Once she found out the results, she requested the documents be destroyed. My job was to destroy the documents, but I kept yours along with others. It's just something about a woman hiding a child from a man that makes me sick. Then I was at the hospital the day you took Rachel off life support. I volunteered in the records department and was processing her death certificate and noticed your name. Skeet Daubs is not a name you just forget. After some sleepless nights, I had to bring this information to you. It won't bring Rachel back or fill the void of losing her, but you deserve to know your child."

Skeet opened the envelope and observed the date of the DNA test. It was the year Rena was born. He did the math, remembering years ago when Yasmine pulled him into her lustful trap.

Yasmine was young and drunk the night Rena was conceived. Clarissa would bring Rena to watch Rachel while she partied and did drugs. Yasmine envied her older sister. She was beautiful, fun to be around, and the men catered to her every want and need. Yasmine wanted everything her sister had including Skeet.

When Yasmine was out with her sister, she would listen to her have sex in the same room. Sometimes she was able to catch glimpses. As she watched, she yearned for someone to touch and kiss her like men did Clarissa, especially Skeet. No longer able to keep her composure, she planned to seduce Skeet.

On the night she conceived Rena, she knew that Skeet would come to the room to check up on Clarissa and Rachel. She laid in the bed relaxing while drinking gin with orange juice. That evening, Clarissa was stressing about Skeet getting married the next day. She sat in the opposite bed smoking and drinking until she fell asleep. Rachel was out for the night after Yasmine gave her a bubble bath and snack. By 2:30am, Clarissa was snoring, giving Yasmine confirmation that she would not wake up until noon.

As predicted, in the middle of the night, Skeet arrived at the hotel drunk after celebrating at his bachelor party. He retrieved the room number and key from the clerk he knew well and headed to the room. With every step he anticipated the confrontation he would receive from Clarissa. But he had to try and defuse things so she would not crash his wedding.

Deep down he wished that Clarissa was together enough to be his bride, but he had to move on and settle for Janay, who had all the qualities he wanted from Clarissa. She supported him, was submissive, nurturing, was smart, kept things in order, and the bonus was that she was a freak in the bedroom. Skeet knew eventually he would grow to love her. He would rather have a relationship that met his needs and business than being heartbroken by Clarissa.

Skeet entered the dark hotel room loudly stumbling. Yasmine stood in one of the corners of the room waiting for the right moment to make her move. That morning for the first time in years, she saw that Skeet was off his game. Not bothering to turn the light on, he plopped down on the first bed next to Rachel who did not budge.

A smile crept upon Yasmine's face in satisfaction of Skeet's intoxication. She knew it would be simple to seduce the drunken man, especially in a dark room. She wore a short gown that hugged her curvy body with no panties. Her body ached for him.

Skeet mumbled drunken words as he kicked off his shoes and slid out his pants, still lying on his back on the bed. The moonlight sent a ray into the room giving her a nice view of the dick imprint on his boxers. Yasmine gave the room one more evaluation before making her move.

She crept out the darkness and walked slowly over to Skeet. She could smell his cologne mixed in with the tequila he consumed. Now at the foot of the bed, she placed her hand on his ankle and slid her hand up his leg. When she reached his manhood, it was semi-erect. She reached inside his boxers, releasing him before kneeling and welcoming him inside her warm mouth.

Skeet let out a low moan, still not opening his eyes he whispered, "Baby, I thought we were going to argue."

Yasmine imagined his dick was a cherry popsicle. She began slurping and got so carried away, she almost forgot her sister and niece were in the room.

Overwhelmed with pleasure, Skeet continued to let out low moans. He could not believe that Clarissa flipped the script because she never gave head. He began grinding in a circular motion welcoming the thrust of Yasmine's tongue.

Once he was fully erect, she positioned herself on top of him. The ray of the moonlight only displayed her hard nipples as she eased herself onto his dick. She winced as he filled her up to capacity. She began to gyrate slowly.

Skeet matched her rhythm but noticed that Clarissa was tighter than usual. When he looked at her full breast, they seemed slightly darker, but he assumed he was tripping.

When Yasmine's juices were flowing. Skeet flipped her body down to the floor and turned her around face down. He pulled her waist toward him, making her back arch and began thrusting aggressively. In pure ecstasy, he mumbled sexy words as he began to reach his climax. "You're so juicy. I'm getting ready to cum in this pussy," he whispered.

Reaching his climax, he began to sober up. At that point, he noticed Clarissa's ass seemed plumper. Skeet's thrust slowed all the way down and he grabbed her hair and pulled her head back to kiss her. The sight of Yasmine's face brought him back to reality. They stared at each other for several seconds.

"What the fuck are you doing?" whispered Skeet to Yasmine, clenching his teeth?

Yasmine was lost for words, so she began to roll her waist in a circle motion. Skeet knew it was wrong, but it felt good being inside of her. How could something that was so wrong feel so good. He wanted to punish her. He began to thrust her roughly.

"Oh, so you want to get fucked, you sneaky bitch." He thrust a few more times and pulled out as his juices released.

He left her on the floor and dressed quickly before leaving. When the door shut, Yasmine checked the time, it was 4:00am. She peeled herself from the floor and went into the restroom to get cleaned up. She felt no regrets and would do it again. Exhausted, she laid next to her sister and thought about Skeet until she fell asleep. When Clarissa awakened, she smelled his cologne on the bed with Rachel and assumed he stopped in to check on them.

Janice stood watching Skeet daydream for several minutes.

"Is everything okay?" interrupted Lada, now standing next to Janice. Skeet came out his trance and handed his mother the envelope.

As she reviewed the documents, Janice handed Skeet her card. "Call me anytime, for anything, and I mean anything." She walked away making sure to add an extra switch in her step.

HONOR THY MOTHER

In San Diego, California, Roxanne exited the plane holding her son who was asleep. When she made it off the ramp, she found the luggage bin and waited patiently for her suitcase. After retrieving it, she hurried through the crowd and exited the door to find Lenny waiting on her by the curb.

Seeing Roxanne in the flesh made him feel mixed emotions. When he received the call from her two days ago, he thought it was a prank but could not hang up the phone. Even when Roxanne instructed him to pick her up from the airport, Lenny still did not truly believe it was her. Meeting her and seeing her face was all the validation he needed.

While regaining her memory, Roxanne remembered Lenny and his cell phone number that he never changed. She needed her mother and knew that Lenny could lead her there. Zak was giving her small bits of her life, but her memory was coming back fast, and he was not around to help fill in the blanks. She had so many questions. Why was she attacked? Why was her son not able to meet his father? And most of all, why did she need a fake identity? She saved the spending money that Zak was giving her while researching the cost of catching a flight back to the United States. When the time was right, everything fell into place and now she was standing in front of a familiar face.

Lenny embraced her for several seconds. "Roxanne, it's really you. This is going to make your mother better," he said, grabbing her luggage and putting it inside the trunk.

"Roxanne must be my real name," she thought to herself as she secured David in the car seat.

Once Lenny was in the car, he looked back once more at Roxanne. It was really her. He put the car in drive, then exited the airport.

They drove for several minutes in silence before Roxanne questioned, "You said that my mother seeing me will make her better. Is she sick?"

Lenny looked in the rearview mirror and returned his eyes to the road before responding, "She sobered up after losing you. She relocated from Baton City and tried to live the life that would make you proud. I ended up joining her once my nasty divorce was over. Everything was going well until a month ago when she was diagnosed with stage four cancer. She has been refusing chemotherapy because she wanted to join you in eternity. When she sees that you are alive and her grandson, I know she will start the treatments and fight for her life."

"Wait, I am presumed dead? Where and what happened?"

Without answering, Lenny turned up the radio and continued down the highway. A half hour later, he exited the highway and drove down a long busy road. Roxanne admired the beautiful beach homes.

When Lenny parked, he turned off the car and said, "Come inside and see your mother. We are going to get you settled in and I will help you fill in the blanks."

Roxanne took sleeping David out of the car seat and followed Lenny inside. When she entered the house, she admired the various paintings, not realizing they were her actual work. Lenny observed her reaction, he wondered if she remembered them.

After looking at each painting, Roxanne turned to Lenny. "Take me to my mother."

Lenny led the way and Roxanne followed him down the long hallway. She held her baby tight, anticipating seeing her mother again. She only had a photo that Zak gave her. Lenny stopped at the doorway observing Sandy sitting in her chair holding a photo of Roxanne in her hand.

"Sandy, remember I told you I received a strange call the other night that I needed to follow up on. Well, here is what came of it." Lenny stepped to the side giving her a clear view of Roxanne.

It was like seeing a ghost in the doorway. Sandy had seen visions of her daughter in the past that would last for a few seconds. But this time the vision did not go away, and she had to question her reality. "Dammit, Lenny, did you kill yourself after I died? I told you not to do that?"

Lenny released a chuckle before responding, "No, Sandy, this is real."

"Mom, it's really me, I did not die," Roxanne intervened.

She walked over to her mother. Sandy was weak but she struggled to stand. She embraced Roxanne and when she smelled the scent of the shampoo she had been using since she was a little girl, she burst into tears. "My God! My baby girl, it is really you." She embraced Roxanne until she could no longer stand. Instead of sitting, she allowed her body to slide to the floor. Lenny tried to help her up, but she shooed him away. She held Roxanne's hand and looked up at her with tear filled eyes. "Baby, I am sorry. I was a horrible mother to you, please forgive me. I believe this is God giving us another chance."

Roxanne kneeled to her mother. "This is our second chance, mother. Lenny told me you were sick. Now that I am here, could you please continue to fight? I promise I will stay with you through it all, we need you."

Sandy focused on her grandson as he slept. He was a splitting image of Kay'Ron. Sandy kept in touch with him, and he faithfully sent her money every week. She did not tell him she was sick because it would be like losing the only thing he had of Roxanne.

"My precious grandson needs to meet his father," spoke Sandy.

"I know, mother, we will get to that. But right now, I want to focus on me and you. We need to call the doctor and get your chemo started."

Lenny checked his watch before interrupting, "Ladies, it's time for lunch and Sandy your medication. Let's lay David down in one of the guest bedrooms. Roxanne, I had the cook make all your favorite foods." He helped Sandy from the floor.

Everyone exited and went to one of the guest suites to lay David down. When Roxanne was sure he was still sound asleep, Lenny handed her one of the video monitors he kept in all the rooms of the house just in case Sandy needed him.

They went to the kitchen and the cook escorted them to the screened in deck with a beautiful view of Mission Beach. They all took a seat.

"You want to fill in the blanks, so let's start with what you remember," said Sandy, grabbing her a plate from the stack on the table.

"My memory comes back in bits and pieces. I remember you, Lenny's name and number, and pieces of the warehouse where I was attacked."

"So, you don't remember me being a horrible mother to you?" questioned Sandy.

"I don't remember anything else right now, but if I did remember that I would still want to be here," responded Roxanne.

"I don't know, Roxanne, you were so angry with me. I would not have sobered up if I didn't think you were dead. How does that make you feel?" said Sandy.

"Momma, this is a new beginning for the both of us. Let's just thank God and embrace it. If I get those memories back and I start resenting you, then we can go to counseling. But you must promise me you will do the chemotherapy," insisted Roxanne, helping herself to a croissant.

"Well with that being said, let's dig in and get those blanks filled in," said Lenny, grabbing the lid off the pot of oxtails.

When Roxanne caught a whiff of the oxtails, a memory of the man flashed in her mind. She sat and allowed the memory to play.

When several minutes passed, Sandy spoke with great concern, "Honey, are you okay? Oxtails used to be your favorite."

Roxanne blinked twice, bringing herself back to reality. "Was I abducted from a house? I remember cooking oxtails and relaxing. Then the man came into the house and took me at gun point."

"Yes, you were abducted from your house. And now that you mentioned it, there was a pot on the stove of burnt oxtails. You were cooking them the day it happened," responded Lenny.

"It could have been several people hating you. You are young, beautiful, and won the man's heart you wanted. You have a business and were planning a wedding," Sandy said.

David awakened and Sandy instructed the maid to go change him before bringing him to join them. For the next few hours, they sat on the deck. Lenny and Sandy took turns explaining to Roxanne everything about her life until the day she was presumed dead.

"I know Kay'Ron is hurting. Maybe you should contact him," said Sandy, holding David, she gave him a kiss on the head before returning her focus to Roxanne. "Knowing you are alive will be life changing for that man. He truly loves you. Ever since you have been gone it has been hard for him."

Lenny slid the cell phone over to her. The contact 'Kay'Ron' was already displayed. All she needed to do was push the button. "I think I should wait a while. We don't know why this happened to me in the first place."

"That's the Roxanne I know, a thinker," Lenny complimented.

'Don't worry. He loves you, honey. He will be shocked, but he loves you and deserves to see his son," said Sandy.

Roxanne placed her hand on the phone. "This is it. I will meet the man that I was spending the rest of my life with that I barely know now," said Roxanne. She looked at David and pressed the button.

The phone rang twice before Kay'Ron answered, "Hello, Sandy."

PARTNERS IN CRIME

The smell of coffee brewing and bacon frying awakened Rena from her peaceful sleep. She sat up and stretched before easing out the bed. She went into the bathroom, looked in the mirror, and began examining herself. She was gaining weight at a fast pace. Over the past couple months, she blamed it on Kay'Ron's cooking until she began having morning sickness. A week ago, she took a pregnancy test and it read positive. When she told Kay'Ron, he immediately took her to the emergency room where the nurse confirmed the pregnancy.

Ever since then, he was staying close, checking on her at the boutique, preparing her meals, rubbing her feet, making love to her every night. Kay'Ron made a promise to himself that he was going to do things right this time. He wanted to be with Rena, but he would not make it official until he worked out a few issues like Sarah and Shawneece.

"Baby, is everything okay?" questioned Kay'Ron, opening the bathroom door.

"Nothing, but I am starting to look pregnant. I am going to have to tell my father and grandma soon," answered Rena still examining herself in the mirror.

At that moment, she planned to announce it at family dinner Sunday. She was not sure how Skeet would react. Ever since he found out she was his daughter he had been very overprotective. He called her multiple times a day and insisted on installing a tracking device on her vehicle. He wanted her to move into the mansion, but Rena loved her independence. She was starting a new life and enjoying every moment. Lada would be happy for her. She was sure Borya, and her grandfather had done background checks and would be the first in line to get Kay'Ron if he messed up. That sinister thought made her smile. It felt good to have people that cared and were willing to protect her.

"What are you smiling about?" questioned Kay'Ron.

He stood behind her, wrapped his arm around her, and began rubbing her belly. He used to do this with Roxanne. Damn he missed her. Every time he thought about her, he could still feel the sharp pain in his chest. It was the void she left in his heart, and it would never be filled by anyone.

"Things have been coming together the past few months. I have stability, love, and a family that supports me. I am getting a college degree and now I will be a mother," said Rena.

"You deserve it all, you have been through so much. Don't question it, just embrace it. I remember fighting to get out the hood, some days it seemed like a losing battle. But just as fast as you find happiness it can all be taken with tragedy, so enjoy every moment," said Kay'Ron.

Rena turned to kiss him. Kay'Ron was nothing but loving, supportive, consistent, and most of all honest. Rena knew about Sarah and Shawneece and the complexity of the situations. It worried her but Kay'Ron's consistency motivated her, so she trusted he would handle them. But Sarah and Shawneece learning about the baby would be like dropping an atomic bomb on the possessive women.

"Come on, let's eat before the food gets cold," said Kay'Ron, leading her from the bathroom.

They took a seat at the kitchen table, blessed the food, and began eating. Kay'Ron looked up from his plate at Rena and saw an image of Roxanne. He had been seeing hallucinations of her lately. Was it because Rena reminded him so much of her? They shared the same humble spirit.

His thoughts were disturbed by his phone vibrating. When he looked at the ID, it was Sandy's number again. Kay'Ron had been receiving calls from Sandy's number. However, when he answered, no one said anything or just hung up. Concerned, Kay'Ron called and texted several times, receiving no answer or response. He ended up calling Lenny. He assured him that everything was fine, and that Sandy was going through the motions about Roxanne.

He planned to take a trip to California but once Rena found out she was pregnant, he was not leaving her side. He allowed the call to go to voicemail and made a mental note to schedule a short trip. He would just have to take Rena with him because he was not leaving her until this baby was born.

Maybe this was a sign to keep him focused on the search for who was responsible for Roxanne's death. He had come to a dead end and Baton City was too small for no information to surface. Now he was sure it was someone very close to him.

In the Walmart parking lot, Sarah parked her fire red Jaguar next to Shawneece's Lexus truck. They made eye contact before exiting, meeting each other halfway. This was the first time the ladies had laid eyes on each other. Sarah took full inventory of her competition. She had to confess Shawneece was giving her a run for her money. Her face was pretty, and her body was banging like she had never had a baby.

Shawneece was also checking the woman out that had a hold of both the men she held intimate relationships with. She remembered finding photos and letters between Sarah and her ex-husband Marvin. She would never forget the woman that had her man's heart. He would have left her for Sarah if she was not in love with Kay'Ron. Shawneece knew exactly what she was doing when pursuing Kay'Ron.

No, she did not want Marvin's tired ass anymore, but it was something about knowing another woman could have had your man that makes you competitive. The need to get one up on Sarah was a must. Having a baby with Kay'Ron was not enough, she had to come back harder and earn his heart like Sarah had Marvin's.

"Oh, so Kay'Ron likes his women super thick I see. No wonder it's hard for a slim-thick woman like me to keep him at home. Maybe I should start eating his good ass cooking more," she taunted.

Sarah smirked. Bitches had nothing else to come for but her full-figured coke bottle shape. She wondered if Shawneece could tell she was carrying a baby. "Kay'Ron's a greedy man, I must keep him full." She began shaking her long thick natural hair while swirling her hips and ass in a playful manner.

Shawneece rolled her eyes. "Well, obviously between you keeping him full and him filling me up this little girl Rena has his attention."

"Yeah so. Kay'Ron has always been a cheater. He loves new pussy, and this too shall pass," responded Sarah.

"Well, that new pussy has a new baby growing inside," said Shawneece, folding her arms. She witnessed Sarah's face change from clever to chloric because she knew nothing about a pregnancy.

But now it made sense why Kay'Ron was acting funny with her again. "Is this shit factual or an assumption?" Sarah questioned.

"Oh, it's a fact! I have a homegirl that works at the hospital. She was in the emergency room the night Kay'Ron and Rena came in. My friend Teo that works at Natty's said that Kay'Ron has been flaunting some new chick around. Treating her like a queen, rolling out the red carpet, being the best man he can be," said Shawneece.

"This is a problem," responded Sarah.

"Don't worry, I have this covered, this shit is getting handled tonight. I just need you to figure out a way to distract Kay'Ron." Shawneece got into her truck, started it, and backed out of the parking spot leaving Sarah standing alone.

Sarah waited until she was out of sight before getting inside her car and driving away. As she drove, she thought hard about how to flip this situation to her favor. Shawneece was only using her to distract Kay'Ron and once Rena was out the picture, she would resume being her competition. Sarah was not sure what Shawneece had planned, but whatever it was, she planned to flip it by making sure Kay'Ron found out she was responsible for it.

At the mansion, Rachel sat on the balcony enjoying the cool September air. Since waking up from her coma, the balcony off her bedroom had become her favorite spot. Every day she spent hours on the balcony reading books and writing poems as she enjoyed the beautiful scenery. Her father made sure she had everything she wanted and needed. But as she regained her memories, she yearned to go beyond the walls of the beautiful estate.

Rachel began daydreaming about Stellan again. He was one of the first things she remembered when she started regaining her memories. It pained Rachel to think he was probably somewhere hurting wondering where she was. She needed to find him so they could run away together and start new lives. The possibilities of reuniting with Stellan and living happily ever after seemed so far away from her grasp.

From his office window, Skeet watched his daughter. He had all access to her electronic devices and knew she was searching for Stellan. He went to his desk and retrieved the card Janice gave him. He dialed her phone number.

Janice answered on the first ring, "Well, hello! Thought you forgot about me."

Skeet blushed. "Oh, if I knew you were waiting for my call I would have called much sooner. I never want to leave a beautiful woman waiting."

Janice was flattered. From the first time she laid eyes on Skeet in person, she was drawn to his energy. It was going to be hard to stick to the plan. She found herself wanting him more since that day. It was how smooth the words slipped off his sexy lips. He was easy on the eyes, and she would never forget the cologne he was wearing that day. She dreamed of him every night and always woke up wet between her legs.

Maybe she could restructure her plan. Kill his mother, father, and daughters, then allow him to grieve and take his frustration out on her pussy. The thought of that made her open her legs. She slipped two fingers into herself. She imagined Skeet filling her up and massaging her juicy walls.

"Hello? Are you still there?" questioned Skeet.

"Umm, yes, I am here," responded Janice, still playing with herself.

"I need you to find someone. I am emailing you his information. I need him located quickly. Send me your rate and I will give you half now and the rest when the job is done," said Skeet. He ended the call and pressed send on the email.

Janice laid the phone on the desk and continued to finger herself until she climaxed.

Later that night

Kay'Ron was at the grocery store grabbing some items for dinner when Sarah called. He sighed before answering in agitation, "What?"

"I am at the hospital, been having pains all day," answered Sarah, looking over at her mother Lonnie who rolled her eyes in disgust.

Kay'Ron ended the call and exited the store leaving the basket in the aisle. He hurried over to Baton Medical ten minutes from the grocery store. When he entered, the OBGYN nurse was waiting. She led him to the back room where Sarah lay in the bed faking pains. Lonnie sat in the corner of the room popping her gum with annoyance on her face. When Kay'Ron approached the bed, Sarah grabbed one of his hands and placed it on her belly.

"We still have a heartbeat. The doctor wants to monitor me for the next few hours. He thinks I am on my feet too much," said Sarah.

Lonnie could no longer take it; she got up and exited the room shaking her head. She despised how desperate her daughter still was for Kay'Ron. Bitch after bitch, baby after baby, proposal after proposal. She was always around to catch her daughter's tears, but she was tired of watching Sarah stab herself.

Lonnie wondered if it was her karma for not being a good mother. To watch her daughter make the same mistakes and go through the same pain she had gone through was pure torture. She remembered being spoiled by her parents and being naive to her daughter's father. She dealt with his manipulation, cheating, and rejection. She had been completely focused on him, neglecting her daughters and herself. He was the reason why she never had the mental compacity to leave home.

Some women choose the men they want to love them but, in all actuality, they don't accept the man that is for them. Lonnie was broken by the man she wanted to love her. Now, her first born was being broken by a man that she wanted to love her.

Downtown, Rena exited the boutique, locked up, and began walking toward the building she lived in. She looked forward to whatever Kay'Ron had prepared for dinner. She dialed Karen's phone number and still no answer. She began checking for any missed text messages from her but nothing. Karen had been MIA for some time. Kay'Ron ensured her that everything was fine, this was just how she and Zak were when they were on. They possessed each other's time and acted as if they did not know anyone.

Rena was so distracted with her phone that she did not notice two men and two women walking towards her. Once in arms reach, Shawneece pulled the ski mask over her face and lunged for Rena and began beating her. Rena lost her balance and fell to the ground. All four individuals began kicking her. The other female was Shavon who aimed for the stomach area. It was the longest seven minutes of Rena's life as she laid balled up trying to protect her face and stomach.

"Come on, that's enough. Let's go before someone sees us," said one of the men.

Everyone ran down the block and got inside a gray chevy impala and sped away. Rena lay on the ground in pain, she felt fluids pouring from between her legs. The stickiness meant it had to be blood. Feeling weak, she managed to dial 911 before passing out.

SWAMP

Priest was stressed out. He spent weeks in Atlanta and there was no sign of Jay. When he found the motel she was living in, the clerk informed him that she had recently moved out. With no new information, he decided to stay in Atlanta in hopes he would run into her. He dialed Donavan's number. The phone rang twice before he answered. Not sparing the greeting, Priest spoke, "Look, I need a little more time to find Jay. She checked out the motel she was staying at. But I know that she can't be too far."

On the other end, Donavan used his binoculars to watch Jay in the loft directly across the street from his. "No worries, I have eyes on her. I will send you the address. All you need to do is to follow through with your plan." Donavan ended the call. He continued observing Jay. She was sitting on the couch smoking a blunt.

Suddenly, someone tapped him on the shoulder. When he turned, Lydia was standing there. He tossed the binoculars to the side and greeted her with a passionate kiss, backing her up to the bed.

When Donavan returned to Atlanta, seeing Lydia was a breath of fresh air. They had history. When Donavan's marriage was in turmoil, he met Lydia at a coffee shop years ago and they started their affair. After Donese's death, Donavan broke things off with her. But now with a marriage on the rocks, Lydia was filling a void.

At first, he was still considering salvaging his marriage if Silvia agreed to let Mathew go back to his father. But as time went by, he was getting closer to Lydia. He decided to serve divorce papers to Silvia and ever since she received them, she had been blowing his phone up.

On top of Lydia, Donavan traced his long tongue from her lips down her body, vanishing between her thick thighs.

"You taste so sweet," he whispered. He could never get enough of her nectar.

Lydia gripped his freshly cut head and began gyrating against his face. Abruptly, her work phone vibrated. She sighed knowing she had to answer. "This is Lydia!" Her voice agitated.

"Agent Lydia, this is Agent Murphy. I was instructed to contact you for the new escort today." Lydia placed the phone on mute and released a moan as she climaxed. Her juice spilled all over Donavan's lips, but he continued to relish her. She took the phone off mute and responded. "I will be at the office in an hour." She hung up quickly and tossed the phone.

Donavan came up from euphoria. "Turn around. I want to see that ass clap while I'm in it."

In one move, Lydia turned her body into the doggy style position. She arched her back to compacity, ready to take all of him. Donavan spread her chocolate cheeks and entered her warm wet pussy. He released sensual sounds. Damn she felt so good as he stroked with precision for the next half hour.

When he was ready to burst, he released inside of her and collapsed onto the bed.

"You did not pull out. I stopped taking birth control over a year ago," said Lydia. When Donavan did not respond, she gathered herself and went into the bathroom to shower. Ten minutes later, she exited the bathroom and Donavan was still lying in bed. She looked down at his manhood, it was still a nice size while soft. "Donavan, we must be careful. I told you I was off the pill for health reasons. The last thing we need to do is bring a child in this world while you are still in a marriage."

Donavan pulled her down onto the bed and held her. She melted in his muscular arms. "I know your heart is on the line. Please don't leave me. I sent her the divorce papers. I am ready to move on."

The thought of walking away made Lydia feel sick to her stomach so she changed the subject. "You know what? I need one of your famous steaks tonight for dinner."

"Perfect, I will go to the butcher and get us some good cuts. What time will I expect you back?" questioned Donavan, kissing her on the forehead. Lydia reminded him so much of Sylvia; they even had the same features. That made it easy to forget about his wife while with her.

"About seven this evening. I am training the new agent, so I am off active duty," responded Lydia, standing up.

Donavan laid in bed and watched her get dressed. When she was out the door, he got up and showered.

Across the street Zak tried to relax. He was flying back and forth between Atlanta and Baton City. "Jay, how you like the place?" questioned Zak.

"It's nothing like the motel, but I will make it work," joked Jay, still chilling on the peanut butter brown leather couch.

Zak could not stand to leave Jay in that cheap motel, so he let her move into a loft he used when he was in Atlanta. He wanted to support her, but he was stuck in the middle of everything. He was feeling like a loyal snake these days. He tried to help as much as he could in hopes not to look so bad when shit hit the fan.

"Sis, you know that if Priest needed me that I will be there for him too. I just want to put that out there," said Zak.

"I know, and I don't expect you to take any sides. That's why I went off on my own. All this is my fault. Everyone has tried to love and guide me in the right direction, and I fucked it all up. Now I am paying for it tenfold. Priest handed me everything. We had a home. I had a business, my son, and love. He gave me an out and I was greedy, and full of pride." Jay took a drag of her blunt. "It was one of our biggest fights. The night I shot that little girl, Priest told me not to go, but he was there rescuing me afterwards. Then I watched him break after Matthew was taken. He still tried to save me while he was breaking. I never had anyone do that for me. I didn't deserve him at all. I pray that one of us can get Matthew back and if we do, I will be okay with dying."

"I commend you for taking accountability. I hope things go the way they need to, and Matthew returns to both his parents," said Zak.

Jay stood from the couch and gave him a salute. She walked over to the large window. Across the way, Donavan stared out his window at her. His phone vibrated; it was Silvia, but he didn't bother to answer. It seemed like she knew he was standing there but that was impossible because his windows were tinted. "Yeah, you are just where I want you," whispered Donavan to himself.

The next morning, Kay'Ron awakened and looked over at Sarah who was still asleep. He slid out of bed and went to the bathroom to take his morning shit. While on the toilet, he checked his phone for any messages from Rena. This was the first time since they started seeing each other that he had stayed away for this long without any communication. He was sure she was upset and confused.

While he was worried about Rena, Sarah enjoyed his presence in the house for the past couple of days.

Kay'Ron flushed and got into the shower. As the water jets hit his stout frame, the guilt was consuming his mind. Once again, he found himself doing the same toxic shit. This was his chance to show he was a good man and to prove it he had to eliminate the toxic behaviors. At that moment, he made a promise to himself. Sarah and Shawneece would only be his children's mothers. No more spending the night at their homes. He would move his belongings out to make it clear and get his lawyer to draw up custody documents along with monthly child support. Rena would be his woman and they would live in the white house and grow their family.

This was the life he planned with Roxanne, but she died. Damn it hurt to think about her. Kay'Ron leaned on the shower wall and allowed himself to cry. He tried not to think about Roxanne because the image of her in the trunk of the car and on that table at the morgue stuck with him. His thoughts were interrupted by his cell vibrating, he peeked out the shower curtain and looked at the ID, it was Zak. He answered by putting him on speaker.

"Aye, fam, get down to Baton Medical, it's Rena. Karen will meet you at the main entrance," said Zak before ending the call.

Kay'Ron almost slipped trying to hurry out the shower. He barely dried himself off before dressing in the same sweats and t-shirt he slept in.

When he exited the bathroom, Sarah sat up in bed observing his urgency. "Baby, is everything alright?" she questioned.

"No, it's not okay," answered Kay'Ron, exiting the bedroom.

Sarah sat quietly listening for the front door to close. When she heard the truck speed out the driveway and down the street she smiled. Shawneece had informed her that her friend at the hospital confirmed that Rena had a miscarriage the night before. Now it was time to link Shawneece to the attack so that Kay'Ron could cut her off also. Sarah knew her thoughts were wicked, but she no longer had the same tender heart as when she was younger.

The fact was that Kay'Ron had put her through a lot of shit. He dragged her heart along on a chain, tossing it to the side when another woman sparked his interest. She was always ready and available for his every want and need but remained an option. Sarah was not willing to accept rejection anymore and she was willing to do anything to be the number one woman in Kay'Ron's life.

BREAKING POINT

At home, Silvia sat in her kitchen at the island. She sipped her red wine as she listened to the phone ring on the other end. When Donavan's voicemail picked up, she hung up and placed her cell on the counter. There was no point in leaving another voicemail because he was not responding to them nor returning any phone calls. It had been weeks and the only discussion he was giving her was about the children and he sent those by email.

Donavan was breaking her down and she wanted to give him his way, but Daubs was not letting her get Matthew back. He didn't care about their marriage being on the rocks, he just wanted to continue his revenge on the person who killed his granddaughter.

Shaking her depressing thoughts, Silvia shuffled though the mail. She stopped when she came across an envelope from her father's lawyer, Kris. She hurried and opened it assuming it was more information regarding his estate. She came across a handwritten note from Kris with a thumb drive taped to the bottom. In the note, Kris instructed her to look at the information on the thumb drive and contact him immediately after.

Silvia grabbed her wine and checked on the twins before going into her office. She connected the thumb drive to her computer. Once connected, a video began playing, it was her father.

"Baby girl, I was hoping I had time to tell you this face to face. But since you are now looking at this video, that means I never built the courage to do so. Ever since my precious Donese was taken from us, I have needed to tell you some things, but it seemed like the time was never right. I pray that the time is right now, so here we go. When you were four years old, your mother and I were having marital problems and we grew apart. In attempts to save our marriage, we decided to make it open."

Her father began coughing, and when he caught his breath, he continued, "As long as we didn't bring anyone to our home, or deal with people we knew, we were good. I was enjoying my freedom as a young man. I was running through women like underwear. Then, I met Talitha. She reminded me of your mother, and I fell for her fast. What was supposed to be a one-night stand turned into a relationship. By that time, I realized I was in too deep and a year later, I could not let Talitha go. I wanted the best of both worlds, so I moved Talitha to New Orleans since I handled a lot of my business there. I financially supported her; and she was fine with the arrangement. Everyone was happy. I was not wanting for anything because both women were keeping me satisfied in all areas of my life."

"Then Talitha got pregnant. I was into politics and could not afford anything to tarnish my reputation. A mistress with a baby would be a nail in my coffin. I told your mother, and she did the unthinkable. She insisted I move Talitha into the guest house. I was against it, but I did what I was told. Months later, she gave birth to a baby girl, and she named her Lydia. A month later, your mother demanded that Talitha sign her rights over as a mother. When Talitha refused, your mother locked her in the guest house and ordered me to hire someone to kill her. The last thing I wanted to do was kill Talitha but after your mother locked her in that guest house, I could not risk her telling anyone.

That's when I met Daubs, the man that I found to kill Talitha. That night, I tossed and turned in my bed while waiting on Daubs to confirm she was dead. It rained heavily that night. I watched your mother sleep peacefully. That was the first time I ever witnessed her darkness. Hours later, Daubs appeared in my doorway. He handed me my money back and informed me that when he got to the guess house, Talitha was gone."

"She waited several months before sending me letters and photos of your sister. She never trusted me, so she didn't accept any financial help moving forward. Sylvia, I am sorry to blow your mind like this. Contact the lawyer if you want information on your sister. I love you."

Once the video ended, Silvia sat back in her chair trying to process what her father just told her. Suddenly, her phone began to vibrate. When she answered, it was Kris.

"Have you watched the video?"

Silvia cleared her throat. "Yes, I just finished watching."

"Very good, I have all the information you need. If you want, I can email it over. Silvia, I strongly encourage you to contact her," said Kris.

"Kris, I will review the information and be in touch with you," said Sylvia before ending the call. She sat and waited for the encrypted email from Kris.

When she opened the file there was a photo of Lydia. They looked a lot alike, but Lydia was darker. She began reading and learned that Lydia Stone was an agent for the CIA, and she was based in Atlanta. She was unmarried and childless. Her mother died in a car accident several years prior.

"Wow, a CIA agent. This should be interesting," Silvia said to herself.

The stress of losing her daughter, father, and a rocky marriage was taking a toll on her. Now she had to make space for a younger sister. How was that going to work out if she was an assassin? This was all overwhelming, she needed someone to vent to. She Skyped Sanity who had always been a listening ear and was a licensed therapist.

Sanity answered, her voice and face pleasant, "Hey, sis."

"Hey, sis, I was wondering if we could talk. I am going through so much right now. Missing my daughter and father. Now my marriage is on the rocks, and I have a sister that I just learned about," vented Silvia.

"Wow, no point in asking how you are," responded Sanity, making sure her office door was closed.

"I am not okay," responded Silvia.

"I know you are not okay; things have been happening so fast. You have not had time to grieve Donese, you had two babies and fostering Matthew, your father died, and now my brother is being an ass."

"He has good reason. I just need to make sure when the smoke clears, our marriage is still standing."

"I must be honest with you. These types of situations can be the death of marriages. I suggest allowing him space and time to grieve. Maybe now is not a good time to foster a child either. Consider returning Matthew to Children Protection Services. Maybe Donavan is feeling like you are trying to replace Donese with Matthew."

"I am trying to send Matthew away, but your father has him at Soring Eagle and is refusing to release him," responded Silvia.

Sanity rolled her eyes. She hated how controlling her father could be. "You know what, don't worry, I will talk to him. As for now, you need self-care. Take time for yourself, stop worrying about pleasing others. Find your sister and connect with her, that may be beneficial to you mentally," instructed Sanity.

"You're right! Thank you, I will talk to you soon," said Sylvia. Once the Skype ended, she sat at her desk thinking.

Becoming unhinged, she needed a break from all the pressures of life. She booked flights for her and the twins to Atlanta. She grabbed her checkbook and wrote a check to her nanny and the grounds keeper, paying them for the next six months. The plan was to take the children to Donavan, take time to herself, and connect with her sister.

At the hospital, Lada sat on the side of Rena's bed feeding her pho soup from her favorite restaurant. She added some of her extra healing herbs to help Rena regain her strength. The night she was attacked, she managed to call Lada who told Skeet what was going on. They hurried out of the mansion. Driving would not get him there fast enough, so Skeet flew his helicopter. They landed on the roof of Baton Medical and hurried down to the emergency room.

Rena had lost so much blood; she needed a transfusion. Skeet and Lada were the same blood type, so they gave additional blood just in case she needed more. When Skeet knew Rena was stable enough, he took the helicopter home and drove back, leaving Lada with her. The brutal beating caused her to miscarry her baby. There were hours of pain, but Lada stayed by her side through it all.

Rena had just awakened an hour ago and Lada was doing everything to make sure she healed. She had flowers and plants all over the room and played soft vibration music.

Rena could not stop thinking about the baby she had lost. Kay'Ron was right, just as fast as things came together, it fell apart. She checked her phone, noticing she had not received any calls or text from him. She didn't know whether to be mad or worried.

Lada gave her another spoon full of soup before speaking, "Borya reviewed the footage and sent it over to me. You were targeted. You were distracted with your phone then four individuals attacked you. They did not take anything from you. I could not make faces out, but I could tell the body types were two women and two men. I also noticed that one of the women was focused on kicking you in your stomach."

"Who would want to attack me?" questioned Rena.

"I don't know, but I am willing to bet it was someone that knew you were with child. But don't worry, as soon as you heal, you are going into training. I don't want any objections! I am going to train you to be so flawless, you will be able to take down a three-hundred-pound man without a weapon," replied Lada.

At the main entrance of the hospital, Karen stood impatiently waiting for Kay'Ron. When she saw him walking and looking around for her, she yelled his name.

He jogged over to her, "What's going on?" he queried, hurrying to keep up with Karen.

"I don't know yet. After several attempts to contact Rena, I stopped by her place. She did not answer but her car was there. I thought she was probably at the boutique, but it was closed so I went over to Natty's, and Teo told me she was attacked a couple nights ago. I called Zak to contact you and he wanted me to wait for you," answered Karen, pressing the button to the elevator.

"Attacked?" said Kay'Ron, his voice panicked.

He began pressing the elevator button several times. When it opened, they both hurried on and rode up to the sixth floor. They exited the elevator hurrying over to the nurse who recognized Kay'Ron from a couple nights ago. She gave him a perplexed look, sure that Sarah was discharged.

"We need Rena Jones room number," said Karen.

The nurse made them sign in before giving them the room number. They hurried down the hall to find room 1025. When they made it, Karen and Kay'Ron entered the room and hurried over to Rena's bedside.

"Rena, what happened!" said Karen, tears coming from her eyes.

"I was attacked by a group of people. They took nothing from me but made sure they kicked me in the stomach. The baby died," said Rena, looking at Kay'Ron. He was speechlessly overwhelmed with emotions. Another one of his seeds did not make it into the world.

"Kay'Ron, may I have a word with you in the hall," said Lada, exiting the room.

When Kay'Ron came out into the hall, Skeet was also standing there.

The men stared at each other for several seconds before Lada spoke, "Look, Kay'Ron, I reviewed the footage and whoever did this was targeting to beat Rena and make her have a miscarriage. It was two females and two males. One of the females targeted her abdomen the entire time of the beating. Did anyone know about the pregnancy that would not like it?"

Kay'Ron shook his head.

"Could this be revenge from your past? Or the same people responsible for Roxanne?" questioned Skeet.

"To be honest, sir, I could not answer that, I am still trying to find Roxanne's killers," answered Kay'Ron.

"How are you looking for Roxanne's killers when you are laying up with my daughter all day and night? Then the first day you don't show up this happens to her. You are here two days later," fired Skeet. He took two steps towards Kay'Ron. The men were so close they could smell each other's dinner from the night before.

"Look, Skeet, as of this moment, I don't know anything. For the past couple of days, I have been taking care of Sarah. She was having pregnancy complications and needed help around the house," said Kay'Ron. He knew the information he had just given would make Skeet despise him more, but Zak advised him to always keep it honest with Skeet no matter what.

"Wait a fucking minute, you are playing house with my granddaughter but already have a family?" asked Lada. She turned and walked away shaking her head.

"Kay'Ron, I am a man and I know what it's like to have all these messy circles all around, but I refuse to accept my daughter being a part of your entanglements. Just look at how fucked up your shit has been from day one. You have never committed to one woman and when you decided to, she died. Do you and Rena a favor, leave her alone. Unlike your other women, she has a father that loves her and will protect her at all costs. Say your goodbyes to her and move on." Skeet walked away.

Kay'Ron turned and looked at Rena's room. He took a few steps towards the door but stopped. Skeet's words were the truth and made him feel like shit. He never experienced a father standing up for his daughter before, but he understood the power behind Skeet's words. He was protecting his pride and Rena was a part of it. Either way, Kay'Ron was going to cause Rena pain, so he chose not to face her.

He walked down the hall to the elevator fighting back tears. When will he ever get rid of the baggage? As he rode the elevator down, he checked his phone, noticing Sandy's number again.

When he exited the elevator, he dialed the number and a familiar voice answered, "Hello, Kay'Ron," said Roxanne.

Kay'Ron felt lightheaded. He used the wall to hold himself up. He tried to speak but he suddenly felt a shortness of breath. He slid down the wall, dropping the phone.

"Sir, are you okay? Someone, please gets some help!" yelled a woman kneeling to check on him.

A group of doctors came out the emergency door with a bed and put him on it. As they rolled down the hall, Kay'Ron looked at the ceiling. He was sweating profusely, and his breathing was becoming more labored. The medical staff's lips were moving but he could not hear their words. Then his vision got blurry, and his head began pounding like a drum before everything went black.

DESPERATE LOVE

At a local cigar bar, Karen sat patiently waiting in one of the private rooms for Rena to arrive. The last time seeing her was at the hospital over a month ago. Karen missed her friend and was happy when she reached out.

Rena entered the room carrying a high vibration. She dressed for the cool late October weather in the Midwest, wearing a long sleeve black form fitting shirt, black jeans, and high leather boots. Karen could tell how toned and well defined her body was.

"Damn, girl, talk about glowing up. You look good like you been eating spinach every day," Karen complimented.

Rena chuckled. Karen was still the same lively person. Rena admired how Karen did not allow life's challenges to steal her shine. They lived in poverty and her mother had serious mental health issues. Between Karen and her older brother

Jake, she was left with the responsibility to take care of her. When her mother was on her medications, she functioned well but the same pattern happened. She found a boyfriend and she stopped taking the medications.

Over time, her mental stability deteriorated. And it didn't help she chose horrible men that did not love her back. They used her for a place to stay, sex, a hot meal, and her monthly social security check. Eventually, the bills would fall behind and Karen was left to figure out how to save their family. Zak would help her out sometimes. But even though he had money, he still only gave Karen just enough to keep her around. He didn't care about her family; he just wanted her for his own guilty pleasure.

Rena got comfortable in her seat and helped herself to a tequila shot. The waiter entered and displayed a box of cigars for her to choose from. She selected the coffee flavor. It was the first flavor she tried when her father introduced her to cigars.

While the waiter clipped the cigar, Karen spoke, "What has been going on with you? You no longer work at the boutique, you moved out of your place, and your phone was disconnected. It's like you fell off the face of the earth. I was worried, I thought you were somewhere in a deep depression. But here you are looking better than ever. Where have you been? I need to hear the details."

The waiter handed Rena her cigar. She held it in her mouth while the waiter lit it. She took a couple puffs of the cigar before explaining what she was up to.

When Rena was discharged from the hospital, instead of recovering at home, she went to her father's estate. Two weeks later, Lada and Daubs took her to El Salvador to participate in the Soring Eagle's training camp. The training program was accelerated and high intensity. Rena spent six days per week working out. She was placed on a special diet and learned martial arts, self-defense, and kick boxing. Her Sundays were spent for self-care and meditating.

The first chance she received a break, Rena returned to Baton City. She looked forward to spending time with her only friend, and family.

"I am just back for a break. I missed you and had to see you. So, tell me, what you have been up to?" asked Rena.

"Nothing new. Just keeping an eye on my mom and hanging out with Zak when he comes to town," answered Karen.

Her answer disappointed Rena. She was awakening and wanted her friend to experience the power of elevating. "Well, get ready because we are going so many places when I get out of training. It's so much out in the world beyond Baton City. Just being away the past month has enlightened me," said Rena.

Karen took another shot before. "Look at you. I love this version of you. Yes, I want to expand my horizon, but I can't do much because of my mother. She has a new man, so bills are not being paid. I must be around to catch things when they fall. But speaking of falling, girl! Kay'Ron had some type of breakdown. He was in the hospital for a couple weeks, but he is out now. Zak told me he is staying with Sarah. I'm sure that bitch is loving every minute of that."

Hearing Kay'Ron's name started to dampen Rena's mood. The last memory she had of him was of him never returning to the hospital room. She thought she would lose her mind, but Lada and Skeet would not allow it. The two of them stayed by her side, loving, and supporting her. Skeet arranged for a therapist to visit Rena daily until she went to El Salvador. When Rena was not doing therapy, she was spending time with

Rachel who taught her different ways to channel her negative energy through painting and reading.

Her family was pouring into her so much, she did not want to fail them or herself. She quickly defused the conversation, putting her hands up in defeat.

Karen got her drift and questioned, "Oh, you're done with him?"

Rena gave a weak smile and answered, "Karen, I just know I spent a lot of time trying to keep my sanity. I feel so good now and don't want to go back into a dark place."

"I get it, girl! He did leave you hanging during one of the worse times in your life. Like, who does that?" finished Karen.

For the remainder of the day, the girls spent time together shopping and enjoying each other's company. When it got late, Rena dropped Karen off at one of Kay'Ron's spots because she wanted to be there when Zak returned from Atlanta the next morning.

But Zak had no plans in returning to Baton City yet. He lay on the couch in a deep sleep after spending the evening at a local strip club with Jay. He missed having fun with her, so it was long overdue. They shared the same reckless behaviors of heavy drinking and strip clubs.

The cell phone began vibrating. Zak opened his eyes and lifted the phone from his chest. When he saw Borya's number he answered.

"Wow, you are the hardest man to get in touch with," said Borya.

Zak sat up and looked around before responding, "Yeah, I have been super busy. With the high murder rate in Baton City, the funeral home business has been booming. Then Kay'Ron had a breakdown and I found Jay, so I have been dropping in on her. I know Sharae is ready to tear my head off because I've been ignoring her for weeks."

Borya laughed. "Sounds like you need a clone. Have you reviewed the investor updates on the development regarding the clone project? We are past our targets and should be ready to launch by spring next year. Remember all the major investors can have a clone," said Borya.

"Shit, I am about ready to take you up on that offer because my plate is beyond full," responded Zak.

Borya got serious. "Well, make some room on that plate for two more things. Roxanne identified her attacker; I am texting you the photo now." He sent the text of Carlton's photo. "Roxanne left with her baby, and we don't know where she is."

"What the fuck! She what!" said Zak, opening the photo. When he saw Carlton's face, he stood straight up and began pacing as he looked at the photo.

"Do you recognize the person in the photo?" questioned Borya.

Zak grabbed his keys and exited the loft. He was so focused on the photo of Carlton, he almost ran into an elderly man in the hall.

"Yes, this nigga supposed to be family. But I don't think he is smart enough to orchestrate this. You see, Carlton is too small minded; he is great at taking orders but not good at giving them. He only controls weak people. Whoever was responsible for Roxanne's attack is somebody that Carlton listens to and can pay him money," responded Zak, getting on the elevator. The only person that came to his mind was Marvin. He knew they were strangely close, but it made sense because they were both loyal snakes.

"So what action are we taking?" questioned Borya.

Zak exited the elevator into the parking lot. When he found his car, he hopped inside. "Let's chill for a while, I want to confirm who all was involved."

He ended the call and started the car, then drove out of the parking garage. He spent the next hour driving around just thinking. Kay'Ron mentioned receiving a call from Roxanne, but it was before the panic attack, so he assumed it was a hallucination.

But what if the call was real, Zak thought. Was Roxanne regaining her memory enough to remember how to get back to Kay'Ron? But how would she get his new number? The only person that would have his current number was Sandy. How would she know her mother was in California?

Zak sighed. He would have to postpone his trip home to his family again. He needed to take his mind off everything, so he drove up Mt Paran Rd and turned onto Parian Ridge Rd. He held his breath hoping Kartika's Porsha would be in the driveway.

Kartika was a close friend from college. Just like Zak, she was successful and ran a multi-million-dollar beauty business that catered to celebrity clients around the world. From hair products, makeup, the latest fashion, and lingerie, "K's Complete has what you need." Kartika was a busy woman but always had time for Zak. He had keys to all her homes and businesses.

Zak entered the automatic rod iron gates and drove up to the lavish home hidden behind the trees. He parked next to Kartika's car and got out. As he walked up the cobblestone walkway, he admired the beautiful landscape. After entering the code, the front door opened. He entered and walked through the foyer and the smell of the lavender candles burning greeted his nose.

"Daddy!" yelled a little girl running up to meet him.

Zak kneeled and welcomed her into his embrace. He stood up still hugging her, allowing her feet to dangle. "Tara, what are you doing up this late?" He continued to hold her as he went through the kitchen into the living room where Kartika lounged on the couch. Her laptop was on her lap with a glass of wine in one hand.

Zak kissed Kartika on the forehead before taking a seat on the couch. Kartika sat the laptop on the coffee table and got comfortable. Zak passed Tara over to her before grabbing her legs and laying them on his lap. He began rubbing her feet.

"What's the hardest working woman in the world doing these days?" he spoke softly.

Tara snuggled into her mother's arms and instantly began falling asleep. "It's crazy how relaxed she gets when you are here," Kartika spoke lightly, playing in her daughter's curly hair.

"That's because she knows daddy's home and she has nothing to worry about," whispered Zak.

"Yeah, you are probably right. How you been? I have not seen you in months," questioned Kartika.

For the next couple hours, Zak was an open book. Kartika was the person he could tell everything to. She knew the good and bad things about Zak. Her friendship and love were genuine, and she always encouraged him to do the right thing.

By the time Zak was finished, it was three in the morning. He took Tara to her bed while Kartika prepared them a snack. He went into the bedroom, showered, and put on some fresh boxers and slipped into one of his favorite house coats and slippers. He then joined Kartika in the living room. They ate and watched reality shows until they both fell asleep.

In Baton City, Marvin laid back on his California king bed naked as Shavon oiled him down. He was officially done chasing Sarah now that she was pregnant with a second child. He had been staying to himself lately and no one seemed to notice. Shavon kept him up on all things happening with Kay'Ron and Zak when she wasn't pleasing his sexual appetite.

Shavon crawled over to the end table and grabbed the tray of coke. She put some on the tip of her nail and sniffed it up. She grabbed a second one and placed it under Marvin's nose and watched him inhale all of it. When she felt her high, Shavon grabbed the coconut oil and poured it between Marvin's ass cheeks.

He released low moans and whispered, "Stop teasing me and do it."

Shavon traced her tongue down the crack of his ass. When she reached the hole, she swirled her tongue around. Marvin's dick shot into attention and throbbed as Shavon continued tickling him with her tongue. Marvin whined, it felt so good he thought he would piss himself. Shavon grabbed the seven-inch dildo and penetrated, going in and out of him. His moans were now more submissive. It wasn't long before he released all over the satin sheets.

"Ah, I swear that shit almost feels better than pussy," he whispered still laying on his stomach.

"Yeah, you're coming quicker every time," said Shavon, crawling out the bed. She gathered all the sex toys and took them into the bathroom to clean them off. It was Marvin's rule to immediately clean and put the toys away so no one would find them.

Sexually pleasing him had become a job she was good at. In addition, it kept her safe from Carlton. If Marvin was occupying her time, Carlton did not hassle her. So, she made sure she did everything in her power to keep Marvin pleased.

When she exited the bathroom, Marvin was in bed with a full erection jacking off while watching gay porn.

"I am going downstairs to make a snack. You want some?" she asked, heading out the door.

Marvin was so engrossed in the two men on the television, he did not answer.

While Shavon headed downstairs, her phone vibrated. She answered in a low tone.

"Has everything been good on your end?" questioned Shawneece, not bothering to greet Shavon.

"Yes, Rena has not been seen at the spot. I have not heard Kay'Ron say anything about her when he comes around," confirmed Shavon.

"Good! Now all I have to do is get him away from Sarah," said Shawneece.

Shavon rummaged through the fridge. "Damn, if you run Sarah from Kay'Ron, that means Marvin's going to be focused on her. So where does that leave me?"

"That's why I told you about the sex toys and gay porn. You locked in with Marvin now, even if he fucks with Sarah, you will always be his guilty pleasure at the least," said Shawneece. Her words relieved Shavon. She did not care about Marvin having a thing for Sarah, she just needed him to keep her high on drugs and safe from Carlton.

Shawneece ended the call without saying goodbye. She didn't care about Shavon; she was just another pawn in her plan to get Kay'Ron all to herself.

At Skeet's estate, Rachel crept through the house in the darkness. She peeked out the front door to see which car her father left outside. When she laid eyes on the black-on-black Benz, she went to the kitchen to find the key fob lying on the island.

She hurried out the front door and got inside the car. She pushed the button to start then drove down the long road. When she reached the iron fence, the gate automatically opened. She drove down the dark winding road until she reached the freeway. She activated the navigation and requested directions to an address. Her destination was Stellan's place. As the navigator instructed, she drove thirty minutes before reaching inner Baton City. It was four in the morning, so the streets were bare. She made it to Baton City projects and parked.

Stellan met her outside. "Damn, I can't believe it's you." He handed Rachel her obituary.

Looking at her face on the front of an obituary was creepy so she threw it down onto the ground. She followed Stellan inside.

"Let's go upstairs," he instructed, gesturing for her to follow.

Rachel followed him up the stairs. As she walked, she observed the condition of the place. The apartment was filthy and contained minimum furniture. It did not meet the standards she had been used to for the past few months. But she loved Stellan and would adjust. When they made it to the bedroom, Stellan flicked on the lights revealing a single mattress on the floor.

"Is this where you live?" questioned Rachel, walking over to the window to look out.

It started to rain. While Stellan rolled some weed, Rachel fell into a daze watching the rain drops beat the concrete. It did not feel right here but she figured she just had to get used to things again.

"Rachel, I don't know what to say," said Stellan, bringing her back to reality.

Rachel turned and he was sitting on the mattress. "You did not answer my question, do you live here?" Rachel questioned again.

"No, this is the spot. I hustle here."

"Why would you meet me here? We could have met at a hotel or something."

Stellan lit his blunt. "Why did you want to see me, Rachel?"

She was taken back by his question. "I thought you would be happy to see me. I want us to leave Baton City. I love you," responded Rachel.

Stellan took a drag of the blunt. He looked up at Rachel. As she was standing over him, she looked desperate. She came with her heart on her sleeve. At this point, no matter how he broke it to her, she would not take it easy. The thunder got louder, and the rain was now heavier. Rachel could barely see anything out the window now. She took a seat on the mattress next to Stellan and stared at him while he smoked his weed.

Why was he not giving her answers? Why did he seem distant? This was not the same man she fell in love with. Something had changed about him, and Rachel wanted answers.

"Well, are you going to say anything?" questioned Rachel.

Stellan blew smoke in her direction. "Look, we are not running away together. And having you here is a problem because your mother damn near beat Yasmine to death. It was all because of you. Now Yasmine's nowhere to be found. I am a street nigga and I know that only means one thing. She is dead."

Rachel was infuriated. "What! I thought it was you and me! Yasmine tried to kill me about you. And even after that, I am still here wanting to be with you."

Stellan stood up and went over to the window. He leaned against the wall. He looked over at Rachel. She now had tears running down her face. He didn't feel any true love for her. In his eyes, she was just a young girl with some good pussy. The woman he loved was Yasmine. They had loved each other at their worse. He only communicated with Rachel for answers. When she told him that Yasmine was the one that shot her, that was all he needed to validate the void he was feeling in his heart. Yasmine was dead.

"Bitch, I don't want you! You were just some new pussy! Yasmine had my heart and since you are the one responsible for her death, there can never be us," said Stellan before spitting in her face.

Rachel lunged for him, but he blocked her punches. The two tussled for several seconds before Stellan pushed her against the wall.

"You were a fraud all this time, I thought you really loved me!" yelled Rachel.

"No love here, you were just another piece of pussy," whispered Stellan, his voice devious.

Rachel stood frozen. The man she had laid with, and shared intimate things was standing before her telling her that she wasn't shit. What a fucked up wake up call.

Feeling mischievous, Stellan spoke, "Maybe there is a way you can make me remember how much we loved each other." He opened his jeans, displaying his erect dick.

Rachel was so delusionally in love with him, she dropped to her knees on the filthy carpet and began crawling to him. She felt so humiliated, but she loved Stellan so much that she wanted to get back in his good graces. Every time she got close, Stellan would back up. He backed out of the bedroom and kept going until he was in the middle of the hall. When Rachel finally reached him, he released himself, pissing all over her face. Rachel jumped back and cried as she attempted to wipe the fluid away with her sleeve. When she looked back up at Stellan, her father was standing there. Skeet pressed the gun to Stellan's head.

He was about to pull the trigger, but Janice stopped him. "We don't have a lot of time, but I know you are not about to let this nigga off this easy." She pointed her gun to the area of Stellan's dick and pulled the trigger.

The scream that released from Stellan's mouth would be embedded in Rachel's memory forever. She sat on the filthy carpet and watched him squirm around for a few minutes. Everything was in slow motion as she continued to watch. Then she heard her father call her name.

The sound of his voice was distorted but she could still make out what he was saying, "This man does not love you."

Skeet emptied his forty-five in Stellan. A bullet for all the years he fucked his daughter, only to piss on her face when she confessed her love. Still in slow motion, Rachel watched Stellan's body jerk with every bullet that pierced him until everything went black.

This job would not be clean. If Stellan wanted to die by the streets, then Skeet would make sure one of his homies would find his body riddled with bullets. He picked his daughter up and stepped over Stellan's body to get downstairs. Janice collected all of Rachel's items and made sure there was no trace of her before exiting and getting inside the BMW. She looked back at Rachel; she was still passed out.

The drive back to the estate was silent until Janice spoke, "The tow truck picked up the car we drove and will bring it back to you as soon as possible." She looked back to make sure Rachel was still out cold. "I must ask. Why did you let it go that far? You could have killed him when he told her he did not love her."

Skeet looked into the rearview mirror at his daughter. "I needed to make sure that her last experience with him was the worse. Now, she won't have any doubts about him. I need her to understand that this world is a cold place. All the love and respect she received from me and her family all this time and her self-value is still low. She is weak and this world will eat her alive if she does not see it for what it is sooner than later."

DYSFUNCTION

The next morning, on the east side of town, Kay'Ron sat rocking Kade. He made a stop at Shawneece's every day to check on his son before going back to Sarah's to rest. Shawneece liked the consistency, but she hated the fact that Kay'Ron's safe place was with Sarah. She needed to change that. Maybe if she met his family and they liked her, it would help. She wasn't worried about Marvin saying anything because she held too many secrets that would sabotage him.

"When can I meet your grandmother?" questioned Shawneece as she switched through the living room wearing booty shorts.

Kay'Ron watched her ass jiggle and smirked before responding, "Why are you so eager to meet my family? We are not in a relationship."

Shawneece placed her hands on her hips and fired back. "I have your son, and your family needs to meet his mother."

Shaking his head, Kay'Ron laid his son down in the crib and went to the bathroom not realizing that Shawneece was on his heels. Once inside, Shawneece jumped in front of him before dropping to her knees. She released his manhood from his pants and put it into her mouth. Even though Kay'Ron could not stand her, he could not shake her good sex. In less than ten minutes, he released himself into her mouth and all over her face. It was degrading but it didn't seem to bother Shawneece. She stood up at the sink and cleaned her face up. Kay'Ron zipped his pants and took the opportunity to leave. He made it to his truck and drove away. When Shawneece exited the bathroom, she hurried to the living room and looked out the window, noticing the truck was gone.

In Atlanta, Sanity sat in Donavan's loft waiting for her father to arrive. After several weeks of intense convincing, Daubs agreed to return Matthew to his father.

"Sis, I want to thank you for talking to pops. He always listens to you. I guess that's the benefit of being the only girl," spoke Donavan.

"Don't mention it. Daddy needs to retire from all this violence and revenge," responded Sanity as she joined Dvora and Dov on the rug to play with toys.

Not long ago, Donavan awakened to find his twins in the living room watching television. Silvia left a note expressing that she needed time to herself. Since then, Donavan had been taking care of his children. The more time passed, the more he did not want to be married to her. Lydia was the woman he saw continuing his life with, so he introduced her to the twins.

"Now that Matthew is going back to his parents, do you think you and Silvia can work things out?" questioned Sanity.

Donavan, who was using his binoculars to watch Jay across the way, turned to her and responded, "To be honest, when she left our children in this living room and has not communicated since, I was done. She returned the divorce papers to me unsigned. My lawyer assured me that in a few more months it will be abandonment and the judge will grant the divorce. So right now, it's a waiting game. But either way, it's going to be a divorce."

"Damn, bro, you realize that she was grieving also? You know she is close to our father and listens to him like he is a God, but that's just respect. Maybe she needed to fill a void when Donese died. Then when she found out she was pregnant, she didn't just want to throw Matthew away," countered Sanity.

"Sis, I hear you. But you have no idea how many layers there are to this. I am her husband, and she should have been listening to me, not my father."

"You are right. A wife should always listen to her husband," interrupted Daubs.

Donavan and Sanity turned to find their father standing in the kitchen doorway. He moved to the side and Matthew ran in to hug the twins.

"I still think we should stick with the original plan. It's really working," continued Daubs.

Donavan did not offer a response, he just continued looking out at Jay. She was in her usual place on the couch. He picked up his cell and dialed Priest who answered on the first ring.

"Are you close?" questioned Donavan.

"Yes, the uber is pulling in front of the building now," responded Priest.

Donavan looked down, observing Priest getting out of a white Hyundai Sonata and walk into the building. A minute later, Jay was disturbed by a knock on the door. She grabbed her gun and eased to look out the peep hole. The sight of Priest made her feel tense, but she opened the door anyway.

"How did you know where to find me?" she questioned, moving to the side to allow him in.

"Don't worry about that, we have some things to discuss," responded Priest, locating the mini bar, and pouring himself a drink.

"If it's not about Matthew then don't waste your time," answered Jay, taking a seat back on the couch.

Priest snapped, "Bitch, do you really think I want to waste any more time with you? We are getting Matthew back today."

Jay jumped up from the couch and went over to the bar and questioned, "Are you serious? How and at what price?"

"Thirty-nine, ninety-five, bitch! Look, all I know is that he is coming back. Donavan said that Matthew deserves to be with his father."

"Wait, with his father so that means—"

Before she could finish, Priest pressed the gun to her head. Donavan, Daubs, and Matthew appeared in the living room. The sight of her son made Jay forget about everything that was going on in the room. She left her gun at bar, running over to him with open arms embracing him, crying. Finally, she had confirmation that her son was alive. Now it was time to accept her fate. She caressed her son's face.

"Mathew, I will always love you, please never forget me."

Daubs instructed Matthew to go into one of the back bedrooms. "It's not normal for me to allow this. You have my son Donavan to thank for this reunion. But my granddaughter still laying cold in a grave, so you already know what's next."

"I do! And I am willing to own up to my actions, so Donavan handle your business." Jay stood to her feet and mumbled the words, "Ten toes down."

Donavan fired shots into Jay. When she hit the floor, he exited the loft casually as if nothing happened. Daubs stayed behind. When Priest turned, he aimed and shot him twice. Now satisfied, Daubs exited the loft. Instead of going back to Donavan's, he had a car waiting in front of the building. As soon as the car drove away his cell vibrated, it was Donavan.

"You stayed behind, what did you do?"

"Oh, I'm sure you will find out very soon, just take your binoculars out. Zak is on his way upstairs." Daubs ended the call and began whistling.

To think he was going to fully comply with the plan was ridiculous. Why would he allow Priest and Jay any happiness if his granddaughter was never coming back? Soring Eagle Chapter six 3rd Edition, never deviate from the original plan.

Zak turned the key and opened the door, entering the loft. He only took a few steps before discovering Priest laid out by the bar and Jay not far from him. He drew his gun hearing a sound from one of the back rooms. He eased passed Priest's body towards the back. When he was closer, Matthew appeared in the doorway. Zak fired barely missing Matthew's head. He stood there unphased.

"Matthew, I am so sorry," said Zak, he ran over to embrace him. He found it alarming that the boy was so calm with his parents laid out in the living room. "Are you okay? What happened to your parents?"

"They were shot while I was in the back room," responded Matthew in a monotone voice.

"What the hell did they do to you?"

Zak began looking around for anything laying out that was illegal before calling the paramedics. He took Matthew and instructed him to sit inside the car. He didn't want the police to take him so he would keep him out of sight. Priest and Jay were both clinging on to life and were transported to a local hospital. Jay was stabilized but Priest went into a coma during surgery.

Zak and Matthew sat in the waiting area for hours before Borya arrived.

"I tried to get here as fast as I could," said Borya, staring at Mathew.

Zak took him off to the side, speaking as low as possible, "I went to the loft and found them damn near dead. Heard a noise in the back and it was Matthew. He was there the whole time, never called the cops, was not in a panic state when I found him. I fired a shot at him, and he still didn't flinch. He said that he was in the room, and someone shot his parents."

"Damn. If he did not flinch at the bullet and was not emotional about his parents, then he made it to the advanced level of training at Soring Eagle. The last step is to control emotions. So that's what Daubs has been up to," said Borya.

"Well, what do I do with him? I don't want to wake up and he is standing over me with a knife or some shit," said Zak.

"Don't worry, Skeet and I will help you with him," ensured Borya.

He needed to observe Mathew to make sure he was not a threat to anyone. Because during this phase of training in Soring Eagle, it was not wise to pull a child out. They headed to the private airport and took a flight back to Baton City.

At home, Donavan explained everything to Skeet over the phone. "Maybe you should make that move up here for a while since you have the kids," said Skeet.

"Yeah, that sounds like a plan. I can finally use that house you convinced me to buy down the way. That slow Baton City life will be good for us," responded Donavan.

"Great, I will have my cleaning company go prepare it. Just select the furniture you want and have it delivered. We will have it all together when you arrive," said Skeet before hanging up.

At the mall, Shawneece pushed the stroller around while Kade slept. As she passed a men's clothing store, she spotted Marvin standing in the mirror admiring himself. She walked in and approached him. Now standing next to him, they both stared at each other in the mirror.

Shawneece displayed a sneaky grin. "Haven't seen you around in a while. You must have found someone that could please that sexual appetite of yours."

Her statement made Marvin feel uncomfortable. She and Shavon were the only two people that knew about his wild behavior in the bedroom. He tried to keep a straight face. "Shawneece, what's the point of approaching me? I live my life, you live yours. We stay out of each other's way."

"Oh, I just want to make sure you stay in your lane. Do me a favor and put in a good word for me with your nephew," said Shawneece.

Marvin laughed. "A good word? Do you think it would matter if I do or don't? Sarah has a baby on the way with Kay'Ron, so who is in their lane now?" he antagonized before walking away, leaving Shawneece in the mirror.

But she caught up with him. "Hey, watch how you handle me, remember I carry the bones and will blow your image up to your family and the world." Shawneece stood for several seconds making sure he did not have a response before walking away.

Marvin watched her walk out of the store. He had to do something about Shawneece because she held all his secrets. All he had to do was pick up the phone and put Carlton on it but this one was too personal. He needed his hands all the way in it.

SEVEN MONTHS LATER

It was May, the year 2011, seven months passed. Kay'Ron and Sarah welcomed their new baby girl, Kali. Kay'Ron sat on the white leather couch as he watched Sarah rocking the baby in the custom-made rocking chair from his grandmother.

Corrine and Sarah's bond had not broken, and this made it hard for Kay'Ron to even think about leaving her completely. He knew this would not be an issue if Roxanne was alive because he would not care whether his grandmother accepted her or not.

His thoughts were interrupted by Sarah, "Could you hold your daughter now? I want to take a nap." She stood up from the rocking chair and brought baby Kali to him.

As she walked away, Kay'Ron admired her full-figured curves. The small pudge in her belly from the baby was sexy. Sarah was still beautiful and always reinventing herself. She wore various types of hair styles, makeup, and had a unique style of her own. Today she was comfortable in her own skin, wearing her long natural hair pulled back into a neat ponytail, and no makeup revealing her natural beauty. He could see himself falling in love with her again.

"Go ahead and get your rest," spoke Kay'Ron.

Sarah checked on Eva and told her to go to the living room with her daddy if she needed anything before retreating to her bedroom. Eva was too preoccupied with her toys and continued to play. She was two years old now and very advanced for her age.

Kay'Ron relaxed on the couch and found a documentary on television. He lay Kali on his chest and began watching the television when he heard the doorbell.

"Who the fuck is this," he thought as he laid the baby in the basinet and walked over to the door. When he opened the door, Marvin was standing with a sad look on his face. "What's going on? You don't look good." Kay'Ron stepped aside and invited him in. Marvin followed his nephew to the mini bar in the kitchen and took a seat on one of the stools.

Kay'Ron took a seat on one of the stools so he could see the baby. "Have a celebration drink with me. Too bad we can't smoke the cigars in the house because of Kali and Eva." He poured two quadruple shot glasses of Hennessy.

He slid the glass to Marvin who took a drink before speaking, "There is no simple way to say this. Shawneece is dead, it appears she committed suicide. She was found this morning by the cable guy. For some reason the detectives notified me."

Kay'Ron's face got numb, another death, he was tired of it. "Where is my son?" he questioned, bracing himself for the worst.

"He is safe at your grandmother's. She wants you together before you come get him. But there is more. The officers found a suicide note. She said she was heartbroken about Sarah having another baby with you."

Kay'Ron looked towards the living room to find Sarah standing there. She had been listening the entire time. Without any words, Kay'Ron got up and walked over to the mudroom and changed out of his slippers into his tennis shoes. He went out the door not saying anything to Marvin or Sarah.

When Marvin heard the truck drive away, he looked at Sarah with lust filled eyes. "I see your cute little family now. I guess my daughter is officially forgotten."

Sarah rolled her eyes. She had placed Christina in the back of her mind, especially after seeing the paternity test results. She just wanted happiness and to forget about her mistakes. But if Marvin lived, he would not give her that because she would not be with him.

"Marvin, I will never forget my first-born. But I must move on," said Sarah.

"Well, it cost to move on. So, get over here and start paying," spoke Marvin, unzipping his pants. At this point he was willing to have Sarah any way he could because she had to pay for his daughter's death.

To Know A Loyal Snake

Lada lay on the floor in the back room of her boutique facing her fate. "I knew you were a snake," she spat, her mouth bloody.

Janice managed to break into the store and waited for Lada to arrive. Now she stood over her aiming her gun, ready to release the final bullets that would end Lada's life.

She spent months getting in good with Skeet. They had grown close, he trusted her. Now it was time to execute her plan. She had to start with Lada since Daubs was impossible to predict.

"Don't worry, I will take good care of your son once I eliminate everyone. We will start a new family," sneered Janice.

Lada released a nasty laugh. Despite her pain from the bullet wounds in both her knees, she would taunt her killer before taking her last breath.

"Silly, you think my son wants to be with you!" continued Lada.

The comment made Janice clutch her gun and grit her teeth. She yelled, "You don't know anything!"

Lada began laughing, but she stopped when she noticed a distinctive birthmark on Janice's wrist. Years ago, when she met with Daubs to negotiate getting her son back, he had a little girl with him. She remembered the birthmark on her left wrist, it was a bunch of black moles.

Janice had been good at hiding her birthmark, so she normally wore a watch or bracelet. She even went as far as covering it with makeup from time to time.

"Wait, I remember you. Daubs was with your mother. She took his money, so he took her life. Your thieving, whore of a mother, and here stands the rotten apple from her tree. You will never be worthy enough for my son because you are tainted like your mother," scoffed Lada.

"Don't speak of my mother!" yelled Janice, allowing a tear to fall from her eyes. She squeezed the trigger and sent a bullet through Lada's chest. She stood over her watching the life drain from the old woman's body. She then exited the back door of the store. She hurried inside her car and drove out of the back parking area. She would continue to try and get Daubs, but her next official target would be Rena.

Hours passed and no one heard from Lada. Rena was in town and had plans to meet with her grandmother for lunch. But when she did not call or text, Rena figured she was busy and went to the boutique.

When Rena arrived, she parked in the back next to Lada's Porsche. Suddenly, an unsettling feeling came over her, so she called Borya while exiting the car. "Hey, Uncle, Lada stood me up for lunch today. I am at the shop and her car is here, but I have a bad feeling so stay on the line with me," said Rena, now entering the back door. She hoped to find Lada engrossed in her favorite channel five soap operas. But instead, she made a gruesome discovery. "Oh, my God, no!" She dropped the phone.

Lada's body laid face up, her eyes still open. The puddle of blood that drained from her chest formed a pool of blood around her body. Borya didn't need confirmation, he immediately ordered his assistant to get the car so he could fly from Miami to Baton City in his private jet.

Rena was in shock but knew not to call the cops. She picked up the phone from the ground and Borya was still on the line. "Rena, call your father. I will be there in a couple hours. I will call my father and get him over to you. Rena, be ready for anything." He ended the call and dialed his father who answered on the first ring. "Father, get over to mom, it's bad."

At the shop, Rena sat on the floor looking at the lifeless body then her phone rang again. She answered and placed the phone to her ear without saying a word.

When Abram could hear her breathing, he spoke, "I am on my way. No cops." Abram had been sick in bed and did not notice his wife did not make her afternoon call to check on him.

Rena returned the phone to her lap. She checked her gun making sure the safety was off and one was in the chamber. She began to cry silently as the memories she shared with Lada ran through her head. Lada had been nothing but good to her over the past few months. She saved her life literally beyond rescuing her from captivity. Rena wondered who would do such a thing and tried to recount any signs that Lada was in some type of trouble.

"Hey, Rena, it's me dad," Skeet warned, making sure he announced himself before entering.

When he saw his mother laying lifeless on the floor, he dropped to his knees and hovered over her crying. All the years he missed with her only to get her back for a short period of time. He had to admit she made every day of his life great after they reunited. Now he had to learn to live without her again.

When Abram arrived, he observed Skeet crying over his mother. He looked over at Rena. "Don't worry, I know it's hard but, she is with your son now."

Abram returned his focus to his wife's body. When Skeet saw him, he stood up and backed away from his mother. Abram walked over slowly, never taking his eyes off his wife. He dropped to his knees and began speaking in his Russian language.

Rena could no longer take it, she turned to exit the room to give both men privacy, but Abram stopped her. "Rena, don't pity me. My wife and I had already come to peace with our fates. We made a promise to each other not to dwell when the time came. We expected to die in tragic ways. My fate looks to be suffering pain of sickness. My wife was fortunate to take a bullet and judging by the position of the body, she got to look her killer in the eye."

Abram wiped away a tear and continued, "I wonder what the old lady said to her killer. I know she made it a point to piss them off." He released a chuckle. "My wife and I made a deal to get under our killer's skin before meeting our fate."

"Yeah, momma was a tough one. These last few months with her have been amazing. I wish my father would have let me be with her as a child," said Skeet.

Just like Rena grew up without both parents, her father had experienced the same thing. It was ironic they both reunited with their absent parents at the same time. Rena remembered spending days angry with her father when she found out who he was. But he was only doing what was done to him without even realizing it. A generational curse that needed to be eliminated. Rena made a promise to herself that she would make sure any child she brought into the world had their father.

Hours later, Borya's jet touched down and he was taken to his mother. Artyom, a cousin of the family, owned a local funeral home and Borya arranged for his mother's body to be picked up to be prepared for the trip to Russia.

Artyom and his assistant took Lada's body and loaded her into the van while Abram took all the valuable items. He replaced the real money with some counterfeit and bogus paperwork. Borya loaded all Lada's weapons in a duffle bag before turning to Rena. She stood in silence watching everything.

"Rena, if you see anything you want, this is your time to get it and load it into your car," instructed Abram as he cleaned his wife's blood from the floor.

When finished, everyone exited the building and three men hurried out of a black van and entered the back door.

"Get in your car, Rena, and go back to the estate," instructed Skeet.

Rena started her car and drove out of the parking spot. But she had to see what would happen next, so she parked down the street in the drugstore parking lot. Moments later, flames began to appear from the roof of the boutique and soon after an explosion. Rena drove away. She did not want to go to Skeet's so she headed to Kay'Ron's spot in hopes she would find Karen.

When she parked in front of the spot, the blinds were open. Rena exited her car and walked up to the door where she was met by Zak.

"Hey, stranger, have not seen you in a very long time. You just left my cousin hanging in his desperate time of need," spoke Zak with venom in his voice.

Rena was taken aback by his words. Selfish people are not worth a damn. The nerve of Zak speaking about her not supporting Kay'Ron, who left her and his dead baby never to be seen again. Rena shot back, "Well, I could not be there for your cousin because I was beaten until I miscarried our baby. You remember your cousin left me at the hospital to deal with it all alone?"

If Zak was wise, he would leave her alone today. He was saved by his phone vibrating, it was Borya. He walked away from Rena and went into one of the back rooms.

Rena took a seat next to Karen; she was rolling up some weed. When Karen looked at her friend, she could tell she had been crying. "Rena, are you having a moment about Kay'Ron?" questioned Karen, now lighting the blunt up and passing it to her.

"No, Lada is dead. I found her body a few hours ago."

Karen hurried and finished rolling the cigar before hugging Rena to comfort her. Lada had been a mother to Rena over the past few months and she could not imagine what losing someone so close felt like.

"Damn, Rena, my condolences," said Zak, entering the living room. He just received the news from Borya.

Rena began to cry. Her grandmother was really gone. She had her father, grandfather, best friend, and uncle. But Lada loved and nurtured her like she wished her mother would have. Her cell vibrated. When she saw it was Borya, she answered.

"Hey, Rena, how are you holding up?" questioned Borya.

"Things are starting to hit me hard now," responded Rena.

"Yeah, it's going to be hard for everyone. Is there anything I can do?"

"No, you are dealing with this just like me. I should be asking if you are okay," Rena replied.

"I am not okay and won't be until the person responsible is not breathing."

"Count me in on that," said Rena.

"Oh, so you are ready for your first kill?" inquired Borya.

"Yes, I am, and I would be honored if it was the person that did this."

"Well in that case, I can arrange for you a practice run in Russia."

"Russia? What do you mean?" questioned Rena.

"My mother's memorial ceremony will be in Russia. I am arranging for you to fly out in a week. You can bring a friend. I just need their information so I can get them a passport if they don't have one."

Rena looked over at Karen. "Okay, I will text you her information."

"Make sure you two clear your schedules. The ceremony will last for two weeks." Borya ended the call.

When Rena sat the phone down, Karen was staring her in the face. "Who was that?" she questioned.

"That was Borya with the funeral arrangements. Get ready because you are going to Russia with me," said Rena.

"Russia? I want to be excited, but I don't think it's appropriate."

"Don't worry, you can be excited. I think this will be a wonderful opportunity for you to get out of Baton City and see some new things. Plus, I need your sunshine in my life during this hard time," said Rena.

"Well, don't worry, I will be right there with you. Good thing Jake moved back home. He can keep an eye on my mother while I get a piece of the good life," said Karen before taking a drag of the blunt.

"I am hungry, let's go eat, do some shopping, then go to a spa and relax," suggested Rena.

Karen stood from the couch before pulling Rena up to her feet. She kissed Zak on the lips and followed Rena out the front door. Zak continued to watch them from the window as they entered the car and drove away.

OUT THE BOX

A week later, Rena and Karen boarded the private plane. It was 1:00pm and the girls looked forward to the trip. They picked up some essential items with plans of shopping once they arrived.

"Girl, I can't wait to leave this dump. I am not even nervous about flying on a plane for the first time," said Karen, getting comfortable in her seat.

Rena settled in her seat anticipating the 20-hour trip. She reviewed the itinerary; they would fly to New York and make a stop before flying the rest of the way. Once they arrived, Borya would be waiting to pick the girls up.

While the plane took off, the ladies made a toast. "This shot is dedicated to Lada. She lived her best life. And to new beginnings," said Karen.

For the next few hours, the ladies conversed, ate, and drank before falling asleep. Rena did not sleep long, she awakened and sat quietly in her thoughts while Karen continued to snore. She gazed at the clouds thinking about Lada. Feelings of sadness consumed her. She missed the old woman who had been like a mother to her. Lada had spent time nurturing and teaching her how to survive. She was always available and ready to help.

Rena began to sob as she gripped her necklace. She hated she was such a late griever and now that things were calm and quiet, she was feeling all her pain. She took another drink and tried to relax, hoping that Karen would wake up soon. But while she waited, she grew tired again and fell back to sleep.

Hours later, Rena and Karen were awakened by the pilot. They exited the jet where Borya was waiting in the black SUV. "Damn, I feel like the president," mumbled Karen as she followed Rena.

"Hey, ladies, these duffle bags are not enough for the next two weeks," said Borya, loading the bags into the SUV.

"We planned to purchase clothing here to blend in," responded Rena.

"I like the way you think," said Borya, gesturing for the ladies to get inside.

For the next hour, everyone road in silence. Reaching the Petrios Palace hotel in St. Peter's Russia, Karen was amazed as she admired the luxurious hotel from the outside. She imagined how grand it would look once she entered. Rena kept her composure not wanting to show how excited she was to be in such a beautiful place despite the circumstances.

"You two will stay in a suite together. It will surely accommodate your needs. I figure since this is a new place, you two will want to stick close," said Borya as he led the ladies through the massive double glass doors of the hotel.

While Karen observed the beauty of Patios Palace, Rena observed that all the mirrors were covered. Borya read her mind and spoke, "It's a tradition in our family to cover mirrors upon death." He pressed the elevator button. "The assistant will show you your suite and then a car can take you to the Galleria Mall. Rena, you will meet with my father and I before dinner. We have some things to discuss, like what you will expect for the next few days."

Rena nodded before joining Karen and the assistant who were waiting on the elevator. The assistant only allowed time for Rena and Karen to drop their bags and see their suite before taking them to an awaiting car for hours of shopping.

"Rena, this is the shit! I'm calling Zak as soon as I get back to the room," said Karen.

When they arrived at the mall, the ladies purchased various items like clothes, shoes, jewelry, and hair accessories. They were so engrossed they barely made it back in time to meet with Abram.

Rena instructed the assistant to take their shopping bags to their suite and was escorted to see Abram. Rena expected to see Abram sicklier than the day Lada died but to her surprise, he looked healthier. Abram greeted the girls and instructed the servants to retrieve the black bread and more vodka.

"I hope your travel was well. I am honored you were able to come, Lada would not have it any other way. I know you have a lot of questions so let me begin. This is the third night of the ceremony. We will enjoy dinner and party, and Lada's body will be available for view. Based on our customs, in six more days, my wife's soul will leave her body and family will be here to rejoice this. On the fourteenth day, Lada will say fair well and her soul will exit the earth and then I will bury her body on my private island."

Rena was surprised when Abram informed her that Lada's body was in the chapel of the hotel and that she could come and go whenever she pleased for the next few days. She had to question, "Will her body make other guest of the hotel feel uncomfortable?"

Abram smiled before explaining that his cousin owned the hotel, and it was temporarily shut down to the public until the ceremony was over. Karen listened quietly while surveying her surroundings.

Once the waiter returned with the vodka and bread, Abram poured four shot glasses and took a piece of black bread in a napkin. He instructed them to grab a shot of vodka and follow. They entered the chapel area where Lada's body rested in a cherry wood coffin. She wore an all-white dress and her hair that she usually wore in a ponytail was draped down past her shoulders. There was a beautiful flower band around her head and the only jewelry she wore was her wedding ring, and the locket necklace that Borya gave her for her birthday. She looked as if she was sleeping peacefully.

Abram tapped Rena on the shoulder. When she turned, he handed her the black bread. "It's tradition to take a shot of vodka and leave black bread every night with Lada until the ceremony is over." He handed her a shot of vodka.

Rena took the shot and placed the empty glass and black bread on a table. Karen took her shot and placed her bread on the table before exiting the chapel.

She hated death. She would wait for Rena in the lobby. When she saw a bar, she hurried over to get a drink. "Let me get two shots of vodka please, any brand will do," ordered Karen to the bartender. She watched him pour the shots before she grabbed one and took it. She didn't allow the burning to subside before she took the second one. The hard vodka stung her throat and burned her chest.

While she recovered, someone approached her. "Are you waiting for someone?" the man inquired.

Karen turned quickly noticing that the voice was American and sexy.

Skeet stood before her wearing a white Polo shirt that fitted his upper body well. It showed off his toned arms, chest, and abs. His teal-colored slacks complimented the teal Polo symbol on his shirt. He wore a fisherman hat. It seemed out of place but coordinated well. Skeet was one of the few that made the clothes look good. He preferred dressing comfortable verses flashy.

"Yes, my friend Rena is inside paying her respects."

Skeet smiled as he eyed Karen's smooth skin and natural curly sandy hair. He loved how her breasts set up perfectly in her white body fitting dress that hugged her small waste and thick hips.

"Oh yeah Rena," said Skeet, removing his sunglasses revealing his dark eyes. He had a small crowd of freckles that you would only notice if you were close enough. Karen was impressed with what she saw. She could tell Skeet was older, but he was still sexy.

"How do you know Rena? We haven't been here for a day," questioned Karen, giving Skeet a flirty smile.

Skeet reframed from revealing that Rena was his daughter. He was going to make this trip worthwhile. He was interested in Karen and wanted her to get to know him before breaking the news about who he really was.

"So, will I see you at the dinner tonight? Maybe we can step away and talk," questioned Skeet, following up with a charming smile.

Karen liked his swag and was feeling adventurous. "I don't see any harm in that," she replied, blushing.

Skeet smiled and put on his shades before heading to the elevator so that he could settle in his room.

Later that evening, the banquet area filled with Lada's family and friends from all over. Rena sat at the main table with Abram and Borya. Karen was invited to sit at the main table but declined because she felt it was disrespectful to the family. She found a table in the back where she could see everything going on.

After prayer, everyone was allowed to eat. Karen fixed her plate, sat, and ate as she checked for Skeet. The chemistry was evident, and he had been on her mind since she met him. Karen remembered the same immediate connection with Zak. She drifted away allowing memories of her and Zak to run like a movie. She was so engrossed in her thoughts that she didn't notice Rena had taken a seat next to her.

"Hey, are you good? I know Zak has been blowing your phone up," said Rena, breaking her trance.

Karen took a moment to gather herself. "Oh yeah Zak. He has been a complete asshole since I left. I would probably be angry also if the shoe was on the other foot."

Rena rolled her eyes. "Karen, he does leave you all the time. Honestly, I don't think he even lives in Baton City. He has children and you never met them. That could only mean one thing. He has a woman."

Her words stung, but Karen could not deny the facts. She knew about Zak's family and hoped one day he would leave them and be with her.

"Karen, he is only checking for you because he does not have easy access to you right now. Have fun and make his ass wait," encouraged Rena.

When Karen revealed her devious smirk, Rena knew she had received her words. "Okay. I am going to pay respect to Lada for the night. I will be back shortly," spoke Rena, standing up and walking away not waiting on her friend to respond.

Karen continued to look around, hoping the mysterious man would show up.

The dinner turned into a party. People danced, and some cried. People were so intoxicated, Abram ordered security to guard the chapel. Rena returned and by then Karen was tipsy.

"Have a shot with me, family, and let's party with the best of them!" yelled Karen as she passed Rena a shot glass filled with vodka.

They toasted and took a shot before slamming the glasses on the table. The ladies made their way to the floor and began dancing. Skeet entered the area and observed them enjoying themselves and he smiled. He didn't want to show his face but planned to catch Karen later for some alone time after his meeting with Borya in the penthouse.

He entered the elevator, and the assistant pressed the button. When he exited, two guards stood on opposite sides of the penthouse door. One of the men greeted him before opening the door, allowing him to enter.

Borya waited on the couch. "It's been a while," said Borya, pouring scotch and gesturing for Skeet to join him.

Skeet took a seat and Borya handed him the glass before going over to the bar to retrieve the cigars. He returned to the couch, and they fired up their cigars before Borya spoke again, "I wanted to get you out of the country before explaining to you what happened to our mother." He revealed the alley camera footage of Janice leaving the boutique. "The footage inside was damaged but I have my best guy on it so we can see what went down inside, it should be ready when we get back home."

"A true loyal snake. This bitch has been around to seek retribution," said Skeet through gritted teeth.

They were disturbed by Abram entering. He greeted them before taking a seat at the bar.

"Hey, old man, it seems like the penthouse would be more of your taste," joked Skeet.

"Oh, you have it all wrong, son. I'm a traditional man, the presidential suite suits me well," Abram replied, trying to salvage humor in hard times.

For the next hour, Skeet listened while Borya and Abram talked about Lada. He envied all the precious memories they shared with his mother. He had to keep reminding himself that he was blessed to have her over the past few months. But it infuriated him that Janice came and ceased the new memories he would make.

Borya went over to the bar, took out his silver case, and placed it on the bar. His father displayed a look of disgust. He placed his hand up and spoke, "Just listen, my son, before you go sniffing that shit in your nose. Skeet, your mother wanted me to make sure you knew the whole story on why she was not there for you. As you know, your father played a big role in why you were not able to spend your life with your mother. Daubs and Lada met and were in the life of crime together. My wife was a stone-cold killer. When she was on a mission, she met Daubs who was in the marines. The two collaborated and became America's worst nightmare. They were eventually captured by the government and jailed on an island for over a year. The government needed a job done that only Daubs and Lada could fulfill." Abram took a moment to drink the scotch before continuing,

"They were granted immunity in exchange for doing contracts for the American government. During their time together, they fell in love and conceived you. They tried to live as a normal family, but some heat from their past had returned to haunt them so they decided to split up. Daubs insisted on taking you because he felt he could protect you more. It was a hard choice, but Lada felt she could convince Daubs to bring you to Russia once she showed him that she would survive and make a living.

But Daubs did not agree so he continued to travel making it impossible for her to find you. She was close one time when your father settled down with a woman, her name was Dorlinda. But when she traveled to her last known address it was vacant. After months of trying, she ran out of resources and returned to Russia and began learning to move on." Abram finished his drink.

"Who is Dorlinda? And what made her so important?" questioned Skeet. He never remembered his father dealing with anyone. But Daubs never exposed his son to any woman. Instead, Skeet was taken care of by nannies, and his father made sure he did not grow attached to them by changing them every six months to a year.

Abram took another shot of scotch and prepared to explain to Skeet who Dorlinda was.

DORLINDA

Daubs met Dorlinda in a countryside bar down south when he had to rescue her from her drunken abusive boyfriend. Dorlinda was extremely poor. She lived in a shack in Alabama that had dirt floors. She was barely able to feed her daughter Janice who was a toddler. The two became awfully close and Daubs found himself falling in love with her. He began to invest more into the young woman in hopes he could transform her into a better person.

But Dorlinda experienced a hard life and was set in her ways. She was greedy and knew no other way but to take. Despite her loose behavior and drinking problem, Daubs found that Dorlinda had a talent for cooking. He invested in a small kitchen attached to Dorlinda's shack to help her make money. She began reaping the benefits of the business but still found the fast life of drinking and being loose much better. Just like a loyal snake, she struck Daubs the first chance she got not realizing who she was dealing with.

Dorlinda had him fooled. Sometimes the heart can be stronger than our minds. Daubs got comfortable with leaving his money with her. Dorlinda stole all the money placing Daubs into a financial bind with some business investments. Once he resolved his debts, he went on the hunt for Dorlinda. When he found her, she was in Georgia living in a beautiful neighborhood with Janice's father Bart. He made his move on Christmas. Bart arrived home at midnight and Daubs was waiting for him in the garage while Dorlinda and her daughter slept peacefully in their bedrooms.

As soon as the garage door closed, Bart exited his car. Daubs came from behind, slashing his throat. He watched the life drain from him before proceeding into the house. Dorlinda awakened and came out of her bedroom assuming Janice had awakened. The sight of Daubs was unnerving, she froze as he walked towards her.

"I tried to help you, love you, and this is what you do to me?" whispered Daubs in her ear.

He took the same knife he used to kill Bart and plunged it into her abdomen. He tried to gut her before slicing her throat. Dorlinda never took her eyes off him as she fell to the floor, she died within minutes.

Once Daubs exited the house, he jogged down the street in the darkness to his car. When he drove away, he found a payphone, dialed 911 and reported that he heard screams coming from the residence. If it wasn't for Janice being in the house, he would have left the bodies to rot. The tragic murders of Dorlinda and Bart shocked the gated community. Kyle's mother, who was Janice's babysitter, took the little girl in as her own.

Daubs found that his retribution would not give him comfort. He was emotionally unstable. Dorlinda had crossed him like Donavan's mother. The only person that could get him grounded was Lada, so he traveled to Russia a second time to find her with plans to reunite. Lada met up with him in hopes of seeing her son.

Daubs was livid as he explained what happened. Then he expressed wanting to try to fix their family. Lada took a couple steps back and opened her coat revealing her pregnancy. "I love you, Daubs, but I moved on. I am married now."

At that point, Daubs felt more unstable. He looked at Lada through cold eyes and spoke, "You will never see our child again." He walked away leaving Lada in tears.

When Abram was finished talking, the three men sat in silence for several minutes before anyone spoke. Feeling the high from the cocaine, Borya stood up and walked over to the window.

He took time to admire the view before addressing Skeet, "Brother, why don't you use your legal name, Fedor?"

"My father gave me an alias to use all my life," responded Skeet.

"Fedor, it means powerful ruler of people," said Abram.

Skeet allowed the information from Abram resonate. Finally, he heard the story of why his mother was never around. He felt bombarded with emotions and needed to process the information. He got up from the couch and was preparing to leave but Abram stopped him.

"Let's get back to the fact that Janice killed my wife. We must do something about this. Skeet, she was slithering in your garden, it's your responsibility to make her pay."

With no words, Skeet exited the penthouse. There was no need to answer Abram because everyone in the room was already on the same page. Janice slithered into his life and wasted no time striking. Feeling overwhelmed, Skeet needed to get away for a few hours but first he would go to the chapel and visit his mother.

When he exited the elevator and walked over to the chapel doors, two guards stood on each side. Abram gave instructions to only allow Borya, Skeet, and Rena in no matter what time it was. Skeet entered the chapel and took slow steps. Finally reaching his mother, he began to cry. He was now resenting his father for lying about his mother abandoning him.

"Why wouldn't he at least create a better story," he whispered to himself as he stood looking down at her. He had spent all his life angry with her. He remembered feeling that he could only attract women like what he had perceived his mother to be. Now that he knew who his mother really was, he wanted to be a better man and find someone that he could love and have a family with. He laughed as he thought about Karen because she was so young, and he had not even begun to know her yet. Then he thought about Janice who had snuck into his circle to attack.

Suddenly, his thoughts were disturbed by someone in the chapel. When Skeet turned, he was surprised to find his father standing there. It was evident that Daubs had been crying as he spoke, "Son, I had to come here and say goodbye to her. I told Abram to tell you everything. I knew you would be even more upset, so I made it my point to sit here and wait for my moment to face you."

Finally, Skeet's opportunity to get answers from his father.

"Why did you paint my mother to be a bad person instead of telling me the truth?" he questioned.

Daubs walked closer to his son before responding, "My own selfish reasons. I did not want to lose anymore loved ones, so I kept you to myself. I know how loving she is, and I knew she would steal your heart and you would love her more than me. Son, I have been searching for another woman like your mother ever since she told me she was married and moved on. Sure, I could have just allowed my wrath to take over and kill her or even Abram for the rejection. But I loved her so much that I did not want that. There is only one other woman in his world that has my heart like your mother." He placed his hand on Skeet's shoulder. "I am sorry, son. I am happy that you got a chance to be with your mother these last few months. It made me realize how much you boys needed that. It's like I continued a cycle because I lost my mother and aunt. I survived so I felt you boys could survive like me. But all I have been doing is suppressing my feelings and passing my trauma to my children."

Skeet was speechless. He had never seen his father so vulnerable and transparent in his life. It gave him relief to know that his father had a heart under all the hard exterior. He wondered who was this other woman that had his heart. Wherever she was, he needed to find her so he could see more of this version of his father. Skeet hugged Daubs before guiding him over to the vodka and poured two shots.

"Come on, pops, let's say goodbye together," said Skeet, handing Daubs one of the shot glasses. The men took a shot and gave salute to Lada.

"Well, I have a flight to catch, you know my work is never done. Make sure your retribution with Janice is epic," said Daubs before disappearing into the darkness.

It was now midnight, and the hotel was calm and quiet. Skeet walked through the dining area heading back to the elevators when he noticed Karen sitting alone with a drink in her hand. She was reading all the obscene text messages from Zak and could not sleep. Rena was asleep and she did not want to wake her. So, she roamed the hotel, enjoying its peace and beauty before stopping at the bar for a couple drinks.

"I wonder where my mysterious man is?" she questioned herself out loud.

"I see you waited on me," said a familiar voice.

When Karen turned around, there stood the mysterious man that she expected to run into hours ago. "Well, talk about fashionably late," said Karen, thankful she had a diversion from turning in for the night.

"You look very bored, I take Rena is asleep," said Skeet.

"She had an emotional night and decided to turn in early, but I understand, Lada had given her the mother she never had," answered Karen. Her response felt like a dagger in Skeet's heart.

"I can relate. But I don't want to think about sad things. Everyone is asleep so allow me to show you the night life," said Skeet with a devious look on his face.

Karen was game so he ordered a car and the two set off into the city.

"So, I take that you know your way around," said Karen, helping herself to the wine.

"Yeah, I lived here for a few years," Skeet replied.

"You lived here before! Shit, I've never been out of Baton City for a vacation," said Karen, taking another sip of the wine.

"Well, we are going to have to change that," responded Skeet.

The limo parked in front of a building that looked like a storage warehouse and the two stepped out. There was a long line that wrapped around the building. As they walked by everyone up to the entrance, Karen noticed two large Russian men standing at a large steel door. The men nodded at Skeet, allowing the two to jump the line and enter the building. Once inside, Karen looked around in amazement. The club reminded her of a movie. People danced and enjoyed each other. There were various cages with exotic dancers inside grooving to the music. She nodded her head to the beat not understanding any of the Russian lyrics.

While Karen focused on her surroundings, Skeet was focused on how thick she was. He imagined all the things he could do to and with her. When they arrived at a narrow staircase, he took her hand and guided her to a more secluded part of the club.

"Ayo, my guy!" yelled a man with a very thick Russian accent. It was the owner of the club making his way over to Skeet.

"Long time no see, Lidi, or should I still refer to you as 'Velvet'," joked Skeet, giving Lidi dap followed by a hug.

Lidi led them to a booth that offered a great view of the club before ordering his best wine along with three glasses.

Lidi addressed Karen, "What's your poison, lady?" The confused look on her face amused Skeet.

"He means, what's your drug?" he whispered in her ear before kissing it softly. Karen shivered before responding, "Oh, I keep it simple, you know marijuana, Kush."

Skeet and Lidi looked at each other before laughing.

Lidi waved his hand, and a waitress came over with a silver box, placing it on the table before walking away. Lidi opened the box, it was filled with freshly rolled joints.

"To keeping it simple, and may I add the rolling papers are made with recycled paper," joked Lidi.

Karen looked at the rolled joints and chuckled before speaking, "Umm have you ever heard of Dutch Masters?"

Lidi laughed and handed her one of the joints. "Beautiful, I feel that blunts are wasteful. Besides, you wouldn't be able to handle a blunt full of this. Skeet and I grow this shit on our farm in California. When it's the real thing there is no need to overuse."

Karen took the joint out of his hand and Skeet lit it while she held it in her mouth. Lidi sat and smoked two joints with them before dismissing himself for the night to tend to club business. For the next couple hours, Karen talked as Skeet listened. When it was 4:00am the club was empty, and Karen was high and beyond tipsy.

Skeet said goodbye to Lidi and helped Karen out the club to the limo. During the ride back to the hotel, Karen was the aggressor making sexual advances towards Skeet. He tried to resist, finding drunk pussy unattractive, but Karen was persistent. She sat on the opposite side of the limo and opened her legs. Skeet lusted over her wetness soaking the seat of her panties. Karen removed them before slipping her finger inside herself. Losing his restraints, Skeet gave in but not all the way. He kneeled on the limo floor, grabbed her hand from between her legs and inserted his index and middle finger inside of her. Karen moaned in pleasure as his fingers felt more pleasurable than any dick she had ever felt.

Skeet pressed his thumb on her clit, continuing to move his fingers in and out of her wetness. Watching her moan as her natural juices saturated his hand had him hard as a rock. Karen turned her body around and was now in a doggie style position. She wanted him to fuck her, but Skeet had other plans. He reinserted his fingers and continued sliding in and out while

Karen gyrated in a circular motion. Karen reached her peak just in time for the limo to arrive at the hotel. Skeet wiped his hand off and helped Karen out the limo. They hurried inside the hotel and to the elevator making out until they reached her suite where Rena was still asleep.

"You have to finish what you started," said Karen, holding on to Skeet's shirt.

He smiled and kneeled, giving her a passionate kiss on the lips. "You may want to get a dose of this on a sober level." He slid Karen's key card into the door so it could open. He turned and walked away whistling.

Karen stumbled into the room trying to be careful not to wake Rena. She undressed and flopped down in bed next to her friend instead of her own and fell fast asleep.

BUSINESS AS USUAL

Lada's homegoing celebration was an opportunity for major tycoons to conduct business. Big timers from all over the world were able to come into Saint Petersburg and stay at the hotel. The presidential floor was where all the business was conducted in between the scheduled ceremonies. Various meetings were held at different times to tie up loose ends, share new information, pay off debts, and strategize on new plans for expansion. This was also an opportunity for Skeet to get acclimated into his mother's foreign business affairs.

Abram was ready to retire and pass down his business to both Skeet and Borya so their presence at all the meetings were vital. In between meetings, the brothers took time to talk about personal things.

"I am hearing great things about Rena at Soring Eagle. How are things going with the father and daughter relationship?" questioned Borya.

"Things are going well. But that miscarriage really had her in a dark place," responded Skeet, taking a sip of his black coffee.

"Don't worry, my brother, Rena is a lot tougher than you are giving her credit for. You realize that she has been experiencing pain all her life and she processes things well. I can say she is truly our bloodline," finished Borya, looking at the view of water and mountains far away.

"Yeah, you are right, she doesn't want to be pampered like Rachel," said Skeet, shaking his head in amusement.

"Mother said she will be one of us whether we like it or not," said Borya in a more serious tone.

Skeet looked at his brother furiously. He did not want Rena to ever live a dark life. Borya observed his brother's facial expression. "I see this is not what you want for her, but you will have to accept it because she is going to do what she wants."

Skeet looked over the balcony down at the courtyard at the children playing. He had hopes that his children never had to put their hands in dirt and just lived lavish from his hard work. Rachel embraced the lavish life, but Rena was the opposite. His brother was right, he had to accept who Rena was and teach her all he knew.

"Brother, let me prove to you that she is ready. I have a job to do while I am over here, let me take her out and see if all that training has paid off," said Borya.

Skeet looked over at him and sighed. "Okay, but I want all the information about the job."

Borya explained about a man named Gada. He became a snitch which was causing heat on a lot of Borya and Abram's clients in France. Gada had been a loyal servant to Borya but was turned over by the government to avoid doing time. He was singing like a bird at the beginning, but was procrastinating on giving the feds what they wanted. But Gada was running out of diversions with the authorities and planned to give them the information they needed. He would gain immunity and a new identity. Currently, he was hiding out in

China with no monitoring system and reported to the government weekly.

"I hate snitches. Especially the ones that do dirt then use snitching not to suffer the consequences," said Skeet, his voice full of venom.

"When anyone affects me and my family, I like to handle it personally instead of outsourcing. I'm flying in tomorrow. Bly has been watching him and has bugged his apartment, so I receive daily reports on all his moves and conversations. I will prepare Rena and you are welcome to be present for that part. We need to talk with her today while she eats breakfast."

"Sounds like a plan. Bly, I really like that young man," responded Skeet.

The brothers shook hands and went back inside to start conducting meetings with Abram.

One floor down, Rena was awakened by loud snoring. When she sat up, Karen was at the foot of her bed sleeping with only a bra on.

"What the fuck," Rena mumbled to herself, looking around making sure no one else was in the suite.

Karen's phone vibrated. Rena checked it reviewing the several missed calls from Zak. She shook her head and laughed thinking of how mad he had to be right now. She put the phone on the table and went out onto the balcony. She stretched while taking in the view. She could get used to this lifestyle. When she heard the suite phone ring, she hurried inside and answered. Borya was on the other end requesting her attendance at breakfast alone. Rena agreed before hanging up and returning the phone to the desk.

As she showered, she wondered what the meeting would be about. A half hour later, she was dressed and exited the suite leaving Karen, she was still asleep. She got on the elevator and headed to the presidential floor. When she stepped off, the guards escorted her, making sure she was unseen by anyone to protect her identity.

Borya and Skeet were waiting in a small meeting room with breakfast. When Rena arrived, she was happy to see her father made it. Skeet pulled out a chair and gestured for her to sit. She eyed the sunny side up eggs, chicken sausage links, orange juice, French toast, and grits. Rena piled food on her plate and began eating. She listened to her uncle and father conversate about business.

She noticed that Borya referred to Skeet as Fedor, so she questioned, "Uncle, why do you call my father Fedor?"

Skeet answered, "Fedor is my birth name."

"I love that name, why don't you use it?" questioned Rena.

Skeet gave his daughter a pleasant smile. "I've just been used to my father calling me Skeet. But for you, I will try and use it more."

Borya interrupted, "Rena, it's time for us to utilize the skills you have been learning at Soring Eagle. I reviewed your transcript, and you need your first kill."

"Yes, my professor gave me a list of approved first kill contracts, I just have to choose one."

"No need to worry about the list. Your uncle is an approved kill contractor," said Skeet.

Borya clapped his freshly manicured hands together. "I have the perfect first kill for you, so you will need to warm up."

He ordered a car and the three left the hotel and traveled to a local training spot located in an old warehouse on the outskirts of Saint Petersburg. After a full day of training ranging from shooting, knives, fighting, self-defense, and response challenges, Borya and Skeet were more than impressed with Rena's experience. They ended the day with a meal at one of Borya's favorite restaurants.

"You are ready, Rena," said Borya with excitement in his voice.

"That means that your first kill will happen in less than 24 hours," said Skeet, expecting to see some type of doubt, but instead Rena smiled.

"Great! The faster I get my first kill, the faster I can get the big contracts."

Borya clapped his hands loudly, attracting the attention of some of the people in the restaurant. "I already know this will be my favorite niece."

With the plans finalized for Borya and Rena's departure, Skeet volunteered to keep Karen company while they were away.

At the hotel, the family and friends continued to celebrate the homegoing of Lada. On this day, the belief was that her soul had officially left her body. The casket was locked and there would be no more views. Candles were lit all over the hotel to welcome her lingering soul. The next part of the ceremony would be the funeral service before a private burial.

Making it back to the hotel, Rena returned to the suite. Karen was sitting on the couch waiting. "Where have you been all day? Shit has been weird around here. We were ordered to cover mirrors because Lada's soul is lingering. I just decided to stay inside the room."

"I went to work out. And don't worry, it's a part of the ceremony. It's a belief that the covering of the mirrors helps guide the soul to the next level. I don't know all the details, but I would not be afraid of Lada's soul. But what the hell was going on with you? When I woke up this morning, you were half naked in a drunken sleep."

Karen giggled. "I met a guy, and he is very interesting, but the problem is, I don't know his name." She threw a grape at Rena.

Rena kicked off her tennis shoes. "Wow, that sounds interesting. But what are you going to do about Zak? He has been blowing your phone up since you touched down."

"I listened to the nasty voice messages, read the text, and called him back to argue for a couple of hours. We will probably do it on a daily basis until I get back home," responded Karen in a flat sarcastic voice.

Rena laid back on the bed and looked over at her friend. She never heard her speak in such a manner about the love of her life. "Damn, girl, did something go down between you two before we left because you have never been like this with Zak before."

Karen moved from the couch and joined Rena on the bed. "I just think there is more to life than just chilling at the spot all day. I'm not doing anything beneficial for me or my future." She was tired of the messy love triangle with Zak and wanted the life her best friend was flourishing in.

Rena sat up and crossed her legs Indian style. These were the words she had been waiting to hear from her friend. She took the opportunity to express how she truly felt. "Karen, I don't really think that Zak is the direct issue. But I know that you have more potential than being a trap house wifey." She grabbed a joint out of the silver box on the table. "And by the way, where did you get this box of joints from?"

"From my mysterious man. We went out last night and he was nothing less than a gentleman. I felt like I belonged to someone while I was with him."

"Leaving the building with a stranger in another country is very risky," said Rena, reconfirming how stupid Karen was being.

"Well, this is your family and Borya saw me leaving so I am sure he would have stopped me if there was anything wrong with the situation," Karen fired back.

"You have a point. Well, enjoy and be safe but get the man's name for me please," said Rena sarcastically, laying back down with a smirk on her face.

The ladies were interrupted by the sound of the suite phone ringing. Karen answered figuring it would be Borya with dinner plans for the night but to her surprise it was the mystery man.

"Could you meet me in the lobby by noon tomorrow? I have planned an interesting day for us," said Skeet.

"Of course, Rena was leaving me to fend for myself anyway," answered Karen, gesturing to Rena that it was the mysterious man.

"That will be great. I will see you tomorrow," replied Skeet before hanging up quickly.

"Wait, what is your name?" yelled Karen but the phone went dead.

Rena shook her head and went to the shower. She turned on the water before peeking back out the bathroom door. "Sounds like you have your day planned so my father won't have to keep you occupied. I will tell him to be on standby just in case." She closed the door, undressed, and got into the shower.

Seconds later, Karen burst into the bathroom. "Wait a minute! You have tabs on me but what are these plans you have that don't include me?" She took a seat on the closed toilet waiting for her answer.

"Borya has some type of ritual planned that will take a day. Then we will return to the hotel for the next part of the ceremony. You will get a chance to meet my father also," answered Rena. Before Karen could say anything else, Rena opened the shower curtain. "Tonight, we need to hit the town and have some fun together."

Satisfied, Karen exited the bathroom and sat on the couch. As she admired the view, she thought about what she would wear. Suddenly, her phone began vibrating, it was Zak. She sucked her teeth and answered.

"So, when exactly are you coming back?" he drilled.

"The ceremony takes 14 days, so I have another week to go," Karen responded. There was an awkward silence for several seconds before Karen spoke again. "Just a few more days. I have never been out of the country let alone the city, so I am excited and want to enjoy this time instead of arguing with you. Being in a different place has made me think more about things and what could happen outside of Baton City."

Zak continued his silence. Those were the words he dreaded hearing from Karen. In his heart, he knew that he had intentionally kept Karen at a certain level for his own selfish reasons. Out of all the women he dealt with, she was the only one that had nothing. He used her poverty-stricken life to maintain control and feed his insecurities. For the first time, Zak had no words for Karen. He ended the call and turned to Jay who was preoccupied with playing the video game.

"A Bitch leave the country and think she top shelf shit now."

"Aww, look at your bitch ass in your feelings, let that girl live! Shit, you have a wife, kids, escorts, and hoes that have way more than she does. Tell me, what's so special about this bitch?" Jay teased, never taking her eyes off the television.

"Karen belongs to me," responded Zak.

Jay turned to him with a look of shock on her face. She knew Zak had some fucked-up ways, but never saw him being obsessed with a chick that didn't even have a bank account.

"Bro, this shit is about control. You get a kick out of controlling her."

Zak took time to process what Jay said and she was right. But that did not change his mind. In his eyes, Rena posed a threat because she was taking Karen outside that box. He needed to sabotage their relationship so Rena could no longer influence Karen.

Control is only a defense mechanism to conceal a person's true insecurities.

ESCAPADE

It was morning and Karen awakened to find herself alone in the suite after partying all night. Rena had already left for her journey with Borya and was not due back for at least a day. The final part of Lada's ceremony was moved up to the next day instead of two days later per Abram's request.

Karen saw the blue envelope on her nightstand. She grabbed, opened it, and read the message from the mysterious man reminding her to meet him in the lobby and to dress for a day of relaxation.

Karen laid back on the pillow daydreaming about what plans her mystery man had made for her. Would it be a romantic lunch followed by a walk in the park? Would it be a day club where they would dance and get fucked up? What if he took her on a shopping spree. Anything would be great in Karen's eyes, she just loved that he was catering to her.

There is nothing like a man going the extra mile to make you feel wanted. It was the little things like daily calls, texts, surprise envelopes with soft reminders of a mystery date. Karen yearned for a man to see she was worthy. With Zak, she was always trying to prove herself. But this mysterious man was trying to prove to her that she was worthy of any and everything without question.

Her daydreaming was soon interrupted by an incoming call from Zak. She rejected the call and turned her cell completely off. He was not going to mess her vibe up for the day. She tried to ignore the nervous feeling she felt. Rejecting Zak was a big move for her. She knew that was just the love she had in her heart for him. Feeling confined, she went outside onto the balcony to get some fresh air.

It was a weekday, and the streets were crowded with people walking, concession stands, and cars moving at a fast pace. Karen observed all the movement, everyone had shit to do and was serving a purpose. She looked at the grandfather clock on one of the high buildings, it was 11:27am. "Oh shit!" she shouted, hurrying back inside. She rushed into the bathroom to shower. When finished, she looked into the mirror and began drying off.

"Thank my momma for natural curly hair," she said to herself, towel drying her hair. A simple part in the middle will do. She used Rena's unscented homemade body cream she purchased from an up-and-coming product line HoneyBe Apothecary. She multi-tasked putting body cream all over her naked caramel body while scanning the various pieces of clothing she could wear. Then after several minutes, she placed her eyes on a powder blue mid-length sundress. It was Rena's dress, but it was perfect for Karen on this day.

She sprayed herself with rose scented body spray before slipping into the dress. The dress caressed her curves perfectly offering a comfortable but sexy look. To finish, she slipped her feet into her tan colored sandals before putting on Rena's diamond stud earrings and grabbing the tan tote to match the sandals.

Karen exited the suite and made it down to the lobby exactly at noon to find Skeet waiting. They greeted each other affectionately then exited the hotel where a white Marussia B1 was parked. Skeet escorted Karen to the passenger door and helped her inside. He walked to the other side of the car, getting into the driver seat.

He looked at her admiring her natural beauty. "You are so beautiful." He put the car in drive and took off down the city streets.

When he reached the open road, it offered a variety of views of grasslands and mountains. Karen took in the peacefulness of just riding and listening to the engine roar. A half hour later, Skeet parked in a gravel parking lot and the two exited the car.

He took Karen's hand and guided her up a flight of stairs to a swinging bridge. When they crossed the bridge, there was a small hut with a counter. The Korean man stood up and walked from around the counter greeting them. He instructed them to follow him down a beautiful nature trail revealing a more secluded hut. The man fumbled in his pocket and took out a key to open the door before handing it to Skeet and walking away.

At first, Karen questioned how the inside of a hut would be. She was not into nature activities that consist of insects. But once they entered, she was amazed to find the hut beyond what she visioned. The inside consisted of a kitchenette and living room area. Inside the bedroom was a king size bed, television, and a private screened in porch where a large hammock hung.

Karen stepped off the porch onto the private patio that was equipped with a small grill, a table with two chairs, a hot tub, and a beautiful view of the private beach only footsteps away. Skeet put the keys in the nightstand and joined Karen.

"Do you have any dietary restrictions?" questioned Skeet.

Karen turned. "I'm from the projects. Does that answer your question?"

Skeet smiled. He was glad he could show off his cooking skills with no restrictions.

While he prepared a late lunch, Karen relaxed on the beach. As she watched the calming water, she was coming more in tune with herself. This was the peace she had only dreamed of. At that moment, she was sure this was the life she wanted. But her cherophobia began kicking in. What if Skeet was just using her? He would have his way while in Russia before throwing her away. He was handsome, seemed to have money, and traveled the world. Shit, women probably thew themselves at him wherever he went. Karen talked to herself. "Don't start this toxic shit, just go with the flow, you have nothing to lose."

She inhaled then exhaled. She was so wrapped up in her thoughts that she did not notice Skeet brought her a bottle of wine and a glass. "Oh shit! I hope he did not hear me talking to myself," said Karen, looking around to make sure Skeet was no longer around. She poured herself a glass of wine and continued thinking as she looked at the water.

When Skeet was finished preparing the meal, he and Karen sat on the patio. They enjoyed lobster, grilled shrimp, and wild rice. For dessert, a fruit bowl with a side of wine. They finished their meal and took a walk on the beach enjoying the sunset.

"I can't believe I let you bring me here and I still don't know your name," said Karen as she kicked her bare feet in the white sand.

"What would you like my name to be?" Skeet inquired.

Karen took a sip of her wine, thinking. "If I had to name you, it would be Malu."

"Okay, I like that name. Are you telling me I am your peace?"

Karen took the grape from her glass and tossed it in her mouth. "Yes, whenever I am with you, I just feel so peaceful. I can be myself. I can be happy. I feel secure with no worries. No one has ever made me feel this way."

Skeet was going to tell her who he was but wanted to give her a chance to know him first. "I am honored to be able to make you feel that way. But I want to make sure you understand that I am not a spring chicken."

"I see a couple of grays, but you carry yourself well," replied Karen, now rubbing Skeet's smooth muscular chest. She pulled his face down to meet hers and passionately kissed his lips. "I was not that wasted the other night and I remembered what happened. If your fingers are awesome like that, I can only imagine what the dick is like."

"I'm glad you got that message. Karen, I find myself lusting for you. But I don't want you to feel pressured about sex or anything."

Karen gave him a devilish smile and led him back to the hut with plans to put the hammock to great use. On the porch, she playfully shoved him onto the hammock and got on top. She used her tongue to trace up his chest. When she reached his neck, she sucked gently. Skeet dropped the wine glass and released a low moan. Karen met his face and parted his lips with her tongue. As they kissed passionately, Skeet slid his hands under her dress and fondled her soft full breast.

"I want to feel you inside of me," Karen whispered, pulling the dress over her head.

Skeet placed his mouth around one of her breasts and sucked gently. Karen moaned as she gyrated on the hard imprint through his pants. Skeet swirled his tongue around her hard nipples switching back and forth giving both breasts the same attention. The feeling of her juices saturating his pants made his dick hard as a rock.

No longer able to take it, Karen slipped out of her panties, tossing them onto the floor. Taking in her beautiful naked body, Skeet began hurrying out of his pants, but she stopped him.

"No, it's my turn to take care of you."

She opened his pants, allowing his manhood to stand at attention. The sight of it made Karen salivate. She hurried and wrapped her lips around his erection. She hummed as she savored him. Skeet tried to muffle his alto moans. She was more sexually experienced than he anticipated. When he burst, she swallowed every bit.

"Damn, this woman is trying to make me lose my mind," Skeet spoke to himself.

Karen hoped this was not a sign that Skeet was a quickie.

He could tell by the expression on her face she was judging him, and he smirked. Her oral was like taking a prostitute around the block. She possessed the art of making him cum quick and he imagined many days to come where she just simply gave him a quick one in the car on the way to dinner, or before he had to rush away on business. With that confirmation, he was ready to experience what the pussy was about.

By the time they made it to the bedroom his manhood was standing at attention and this time he was running the show. Karen sprawled herself onto the bed, displaying her Brazilian waxed pussy. Skeet removed what was left of his clothing and climbed onto the bed. Karen grabbed his index finger and inserted it inside of herself. As she guided him in and out of her, she moaned softly.

"Are you ready for me to fill you up?" Skeet whispered in a low sexy voice.

Before she could respond, he dived into her wetness and began stroking deep and slow. Karen was in pure ecstasy. Zak was fucking her good, but Skeet was on another level. She knew from this point moving forward that she would not be able to get him out of her system.

China

Rena and Borya made it safely to China with a couple hours to spare before the hit. Borya planned to send Rena solo to see what level she was on. He had no doubts about his niece but would monitor to access how she moved.

"Okay, Rena, you have your orders. Meet me back here when you are finished," instructed Borya.

"Don't worry, I got this," Rena assured.

She exited the building and made her way through the streets of China. Her first instinct was to blend in with the environment, so she stopped at a tourist store where she purchased a flowered bag, translation book, reading glasses, hat, and tourist guide. She then went into a restroom at the subway station and put her hair in a neat braid going down her back. She found a kami that covered her all-black attire and concealed her gun.

Rena made it to Gada's building and waited for him to leave. She followed him to the federal headquarters for his weekly reporting. While Gada met with the officers, Rena returned to his apartment. The unit above Gada's apartment was vacant so Rena set up shop there. She found a crawl space to travel back and forth through the apartments. After setting things up, Rena waited patiently for him to return. When Gada made it home, Rena removed her kami and sunglasses before getting into the crawl space. Meanwhile, Gada salivated as he opened the Chinese takeout and placed it on a small table in front of the reclining chair. He then turned on the television.

Once inside the apartment, Rena observed the man go into the bathroom and relieve himself before returning to his meal. She watched with disgust as he started to eat without washing his hands. Ready to make her move, she eased out the closet door. Gada ate while enjoying his favorite TV show, his back turned to Rena. She positioned herself for the shot, being careful not to step on one of the empty bags of chips on the floor of the trashy apartment.

Suddenly, Gada stood up barely giving Rena time to duck back out of sight. She stayed still behind the bedroom door as he hurried to the bathroom. This time, he sat on the toilet and relieved his bowels. When finished, he exited the bathroom still not bothering to flush or wash his hands. When he sat back in his chair, Rena walked up to him from behind and pulled the trigger three times. Gada died instantly from the gunshots to the head and back of neck.

Afterwards, she turned the air conditioner temperature down to disturb the time of decomposition, unlocked the front door, and climbed back into the ceiling to the empty apartment. She slipped back into her kami and glasses. Finally, she grabbed her bag and exited. Her adrenaline was high as she made her way down the streets of China, being careful not to look suspect. Even though her kill was quiet, she still made an exit as if someone heard the shots.

She decided to take the subway instead of a taxi to blend. Before leaving the subway station, Rena changed into a more casual attire. She placed the clothing and shoes inside a bag with plans to burn them. She walked three blocks to the business building where her uncle waited. As instructed, she used the utility elevators. When she entered, Borya gave her a standing ovation.

"Nice job, niece, the spies had a hard time keeping up with you. So how do you feel?"

Rena paused for several seconds to allow her adrenaline to decrease. "I know this may sound odd, but I feel a burst of excitement." She took the shot of tequila her uncle offered.

Borya liked her response. He was for sure his niece had the killer instinct. Rena would continue his mother's legacy. "Your father has a special getaway set up for you after the ceremony," said Borya.

Rena nodded in approval. They packed up before heading back to Saint Petersburg.

At the hut, Skeet extended his stay for additional two days so he could bring Karen back and spend more time with her after the ceremony. They headed back to Saint Petersburg that night. The commute back was silent because neither one of them wanted to leave each other. As he drove, Skeet thought about coming clean with Karen about who he was but decided not to just yet. A half hour later, they parked in front of the hotel and went inside. He walked Karen to her room and gave her a passionate kiss before leaving her in the doorway.

Later that Night

Rena was exhausted and just wanted to eat and get some sleep. Happy to see the hotel, she exited the car and went inside. When she made it to the suite, Karen was sleeping peacefully. Rena smiled, noticing her cell phone was across the room instead of laying on the pillow by her ear.

She picked up the suite phone and dialed room service to order her food. While she waited, she showered, finishing just in time for room service to arrive. She enjoyed her meal of steak and asparagus as she watched the night view. Once finished, she had a drink before lying in bed and falling fast asleep.

The next morning, the ladies had no time to chat because they had to prepare for Lada's final ceremony. When they made it downstairs, they were seated quickly. During the ceremony, Skeet chose not to sit in the open for many reasons and one was Karen.

Everyone sat quietly listening to Lada's eulogy. It was like listening to a bestselling fiction novel. Lada had earned her credit on both sides of the line. She was respected by everyone.

She was the definition of perseverance: growing up in destitute conditions, witnessing her parents' murder and becoming an orphan. She got out the foster care system only to be captured and held as a sex slave. After all the trauma, Lada still made it out and paved the way for many. Despite her life in the underworld, she still managed to shine in a positive way. When Rena laid her eyes on Abram, his appearance had drastically changed. He looked sickly again as he sat quietly during the ceremony.

After the ceremony, only a small group traveled to a private island for Lada's burial. Rena met Borya's wife Aliya, his sons Wayra and Abrar, along with his daughter Amna. Borya's wife and children would reside on the island to help Abram.

Rena and Karen said their goodbyes before heading back to the hotel with Borya so they could pack. Skeet decided not to travel to the island. He was not ready to say a final goodbye to his mother so he would wait until her birthday and try.

When the girls made it back to the hotel, they prepared to go their separate ways.

"Okay, girl, I will see you in a couple of days. I look forward to hearing all about your romantic trip with Malu," said Rena, giving her friend a hug.

"Don't worry, we will have a lot to talk about on the way back to Baton City," assured Karen.

Rena exited the room and went downstairs where the escort waited to take her to her destination. Once she was gone, Skeet showed up to the suite to get Karen and they returned to the cottage.

TRANQUILITY

The next morning, Rena enjoyed a massage and breakfast followed by a walk on the beach. Skeet was only a few minutes away, so he went over to check on his daughter. When he arrived, he found Rena sitting in the sand looking out into the ocean.

"I see you found how relaxing the ocean can be," spoke Skeet, taking a seat next to her.

"Yes, I could sit here all day," responded Rena, never taking her eyes away from the view.

"I was just like this the first time I saw the ocean, and trust me it never gets old," said Skeet.

"I think I am going to invest in a beach house so I can get away more often," replied Rena.

"If you were to choose a place to have a beach home, where would it be?" her father questioned.

Rena shrugged; it didn't matter which beach just as long as it had a beautiful view.

"How about you write down all the beaches you want to visit, and I will make sure you see them all. I think once you have experienced them, you will know what you want," suggested Skeet.

When Rena nodded, he gave her a kiss on the forehead and stood to his feet, dusting the sand from his shorts. He returned to the hut and woke Karen up to breakfast in bed and she was the main course. His tongue swirled around her pussy going in and out of her. He wanted to make sure he hooked her because the news that he was Rena's father could be a deal breaker. After reaching their climax, the two laid naked.

"So, you said that this trip has made you think about things?"

Karen was taken aback by his question. No one ever cared about how she really felt. "Yes, I feel that there is more to life," she answered.

"Well, enlighten me," said Skeet, trying to dig deep. He wanted to know everything about her dreams, goals, even her nightmares. He wanted to be able to fill whatever part of her that was empty.

"I want to be a nurse, maybe a traveling one so I can see the world."

"So, what's stopping you from doing it? You are still young, so you have time to do whatever you want."

"I don't know I just..." Karen stopped and realized that she didn't really have a reason other than she stopped dreaming when she hooked up with Zak. She was too ashamed to let Skeet know that a man was the reason she lost all hope and dreams. Noticing her sudden mood shift, he flipped on top of Karen and kissed her lips before ensuring her that she would do whatever she wanted.

Later that evening, Rena enjoyed another walk along the beach. She could not get enough of it. She wished she had someone to share this moment with. Suddenly, her thoughts drifted to Kay'Ron. She did not realize how much she had missed him until this moment. Over time, she seemed to master suppressing her feelings. Now that she had no worries it was his turn to taunt her thoughts. Lada told her it would be some hard days, but she assured Rena to keep fighting because she deserved more than a messy love triangle.

"Why the long face? This is a wonderful place," said a male voice, taking Rena out of her depressing thoughts.

She turned and there stood a tall, dark, sexy man. Rena thought she would melt into the sand.

"My name is Bly," said the man, extending his arm for a handshake. Rena gave him a onceover. He was well groomed, sporting a neatly low haircut similar to the way Kay'Ron wore his. He was not too flashy, only wearing a diamond watch with a tank top, beach shorts, and flip flops.

"Looks like you could use some company," said Bly, still holding out his arm for a handshake.

When she shook his hand, his skin was soft just like she predicted. "I was thinking this was a place you wanted to be with someone special," responded Rena.

Bly gave a charming laugh before replying, "It's your lucky day because I happen to be special. Come on, take a walk with me and I guaranteed you will agree."

Satisfied with his line, Rena joined him, and they continued to walk down the beach together.

Bly was just what Rena needed. He was sexy, a gentleman, had a great sense of humor, and knew about a lot of things. He was Jamaican but raised in the United States. At age ten, he moved with his father and paternal grandparents after his mother was murdered by an estranged boyfriend.

After graduating from high school, Bly's father suffered a stroke and could no longer work. Tired of struggling, Bly became a hitman for a local drug dealer. Soon, word of his work traveled, and he met Skeet who pulled some strings and got him into Soring Eagle. He graduated at the top of his class and moved his family to Australia.

"Damn, it must be exciting traveling the world. That's my goal, to travel and do contracts when I graduate," said Rena.

"Don't worry, I seen your work the other day and I am sure you will be traveling soon. I was one of the spies watching you," responded Bly.

Rena held her hand on her chest in a dramatic way. "Wow! Are you serious!"

They continued their journey down the beach stopping at tiki bars to refill their drinks and enjoying the wonderful views. The chemistry was constant. Bly realized that he had finally met his soulmate. By the end of the night, the two were tipsy and most of all best friends. They fell asleep on the balcony of Rena's suite.

Two days later, Borya picked Rena up from the resort and the two returned to the hotel where Karen waited in the suite. The ladies spent their final night relaxing and talking.

"Why so sad?" asked Rena, lying on the rug next to Karen who continued staring at the ceiling after taking a drink of her wine.

"Malu didn't say goodbye to me, he just left. I found his room and when I went there, he was already packed and gone," answered Karen, her tone somber.

"Trust me, you will see him again. The men around here are different. They are powerful and are liable to be anywhere at any time," said Rena, thinking about Bly.

"Sounds like you met someone too!" said Karen.

Rena sat halfway up from the rug and looked down at Karen. "I met someone interesting. We have a lot in common. He is so sexy and a gentleman. He wasn't thirsty to fuck me, but if he did, I would have given it to him."

"Damn, that's your grandmother's energy blessing us," said Karen.

"Get ready because now we have a reason to go to Australia," said Rena.

"Now that's what I am talking about," replied Karen. Unexpectedly, her mood dampened when she thought about returning to just an ordinary life. "I am not looking forward to going back to the spot."

Rena and Malu had set her standards to a new level. Returning to her ordinary life in Baton City was depressing.

"Who said you had to go back to Zak's ass," said Rena before lighting a joint and taking a puff.

"I know, but Malu has not made any promises. So, at the moment, Zak is all I have," replied Karen, snatching the joint out of Rena's hand.

"Honestly, I don't think a man like that is going to disappear. He could have just fucked you in this hotel. Trust me, if he knows Borya then he will know how to contact you," ensured Rena.

"You are right! I need to be patient. He would not have asked me about my dreams if he was not interested. You know Zak never cared much about that; he just tells me what to do." Karen took a puff of her joint almost choking.

The ladies continued to talk during the night while drinking and smoking joints back-to-back until they fell asleep. The next morning, Borya took them to the private jet for their trip back home. During the trip home, Karen slept as Rena was restless. She was thinking about her new avenue in life as an assassin and Bly. With him, she had something to look forward to and that made it easier to get over Kay'Ron.

At Skeet's, Janice sat in his office patiently waiting for his arrival so she could find out what all he knew about Lada's death. While Skeet was out the country, she offered to stay at the estate and keep an eye on Rachel who declined to attend her grandmother's services. Skeet would have just let Rachel stay at the estate alone, but ever since he killed Stellan, his daughter's behavior had become impulsive.

Janice felt at home on the estate and found herself daydreaming about a family with Skeet. They would have a son, maybe a daughter. Or even twins so she could get the pregnancy and childbirth out the way. "Fuck all this dreaming," Janice whispered to herself as she reclined back in Skeet's chair.

Her thoughts darkened thinking about her mother's death. She got up and went over to the mini bar and poured a glass of Skeet's favorite brandy. She gulped the drink down not caring how strong it was. She had to figure out a way to kill Daubs, Rena, and Rachel. She could hear Lada's laugh in her head taunting her about how she would never win. "I am close to getting my revenge," Janice said to herself trying to pull herself together.

"Are you okay?" said a soft voice startling Janice.

When she turned, it was Rachel. "Yes, I am fine. Is everything okay? Do you need something?" replied Janice, trying to pull herself together.

Rachel took a moment to assess Janice before answering, "No, I didn't need anything, I was just…" Rachel paused to try and find another reason on why she interrupted. She could see the darkness Janice carried and did not trust her, so she spent most of her time locked in her suite.

"You don't look well, maybe you should lay down. Your father will be arriving soon," encouraged Janice, closing the gap between them. She could see the worry in Rachel's face.

"You are right, it has been a long day, and I am feeling a bit under the weather," Rachel turned and walked away.

Janice followed closely behind her. As she stared at the back of her head, she imagined all the ways she could kill her at that moment. Staging a suicide would be easy since the girl was already fragile. Rachel made it to her bedroom. She hurried inside and slammed the door in Janice's face. Both women stood on opposite sides of the door staring through it at each other. Rachel jumped when Janice tapped on her door.

"Rachel, are you sure you don't need anything?"

"No, but thanks for asking. Just please let me know the moment my father arrives. I miss him and want to apologize for being so mean to him these past few weeks," responded Rachel.

Satisfied with her answer, Janice turned and walked away going back to the office to wait for Skeet to arrive.

Later the next morning, after hours of flying, Rena and Karen made it back home to Baton City. The moment was bittersweet for the ladies. After exiting the jet, the two ladies went their separate ways. Rena went to stay in one of Skeet's rental lofts in downtown Baton City. Karen decided to go home to the townhome she shared with her mother and brother in the projects. She had been in and out for the past few months because she spent so much time with Zak at the spot.

As she rode, Zak was in the back of her mind because she was thinking about her time with Skeet. She knew that Zak was ready for drama the moment she touched down. She turned her phone on to see over twenty voice messages. She did not bother to torment herself with the obscene messages he left so she tossed the phone back into her purse. It was early summer, but the cloudy sky made things look gloomy and even more depressing. Arriving home, she sighed. Back to reality. The signs "Government Property" was damn near stamped on everything from the screen door to the refrigerator. A life of poverty and the government reminded their tenants that they were borrowing everything.

The driver unloaded Karen's bags, placing them on the porch leaving. She opened the screen door to find an eviction notice taped to the front door. Karen unlocked the door and went inside to find her mother on the couch asleep. Jake was not at home. Being careful not to wake her mom, Karen brought her luggage inside and retreated to her bedroom.

Across town, Skeet made it home a day later than expected. He had Karen on his mind heavy and wanted to get back to her, but he had more important matters to resolve. He went straight to his office. Assuming Rachel was still angry with him, he did not bother her. He needed to handle Janice and he looked forward to doing it. A simple bullet to the head would not be enough. He would tap into the dark side of himself. He was his father's child and he tried to keep that side buried. However, during times like this, he had to let the beast out.

This retribution would be epic because it had to satisfy everyone. Skeet sat at his cherry wood desk with his scotch. He thought of how much of an asset Janice would have been. He knew that karma always had its way, but killing his mother made him suffer more than his father. He tapped his fingers on the now empty glass. Keeping close tabs on Janice was the temporary plan until he could make the final decision on how to go about things. Skeet picked up his desk phone and called Janice, who was asleep in one of the guest suites. She answered in a raspy voice.

"Janice, come see me in my office," instructed Skeet before ending the call.

Janice hurried out of bed and threw on her housecoat. She went to the office wondering why Skeet had returned so late. When she entered the office, she said, "Welcome back! Is everything okay?"

"How did things go while I was gone?" Skeet questioned.

Janice took a seat on the sofa. She allowed her housecoat to swing open as she answered. "Everything went well. Rachel was in her suite most of the time.

"I am not surprised, she is still getting over that Stellan thing," said Skeet. Janice nodded in agreement. Skeet focused on the partial view of one of her breasts. "You look comfortable here. I like having a woman in the place. Maybe you should stick around a little longer."

Janice smiled and stood from the couch. "Say no more, I can be here until you say leave."

"Great! I have a lot of business to handle. How about you go and get some more rest and we will talk later," instructed Skeet. He watched Janice exit the office. Alone again, he poured himself another drink and continued thinking about how he would get retribution for Janice killing his mother.

Days later, Karen held the phone to her ear speaking, "Rena, this is Karen, I need you to call as soon as possible." After ending the call, she cradled her hands around her head. Karen had been away from her family for so long, she hadn't realized that her mother had lost her job and stopped taking her medication. She ended up admitting her mother into a mental health facility because she had a breakdown when she found the eviction notice.

Jake had reached his breaking point. He had a daughter on the way and could no longer stress himself with his mother's situation. He decided to move with his girlfriend; she was due to have their baby in a couple of weeks. Karen sat on the stairs watching her brother go in and out the unit.

When he got everything outside, he looked and Karen and spoke, "It's your turn now."

Karen snapped back, "It is both of our responsibilities. Why didn't you come and let me know what was going on, Jake! I could have handled it before it got this bad."

"Karen, I wasn't running to the trap house trying to pull you from up under a nigga. Maybe if you were home then you would have seen what was going on instead of being Zak's side chick," Jake fired back, feeling the guilt from Karen's remark.

Jake never approved of his sister being with Zak. He knew that Zak was married with children. The five-star hotel he worked at was the one Sharae and her children checked into when they were in Baton City. Jake tried to tell Karen about Zak, but she refused to listen to him.

Angry, Karen threw her glass of water at Jake's car before storming into the house. Her brother's words hurt and brought Karen back to reality about Zak. Inside, she burst into tears at the sound of Jake driving out of the parking lot. She had the responsibility of her mother in her hands, and they would be homeless in a week.

Karen sat up on the bed and opened the box of rolled joints that she brought back from Russia. She fired up one and began planning how she would ask her best friend for the money. Then she would get a full-time job, enroll into the Baton City Community College, and complete the registered nursing program. If her brother were going to leave them, she would step up and handle their business. But first, she had to figure out how to get out of the eviction.

Suddenly, she was interrupted by her phone ringing from a private number, it was Skeet. "Hello?" she answered, not hiding the distraught in her voice.

"Is everything okay?" asked Skeet from the other end.

Karen paused for a moment to get herself together before answering, "Everything is fine, I was jus—"

Before she could finish, Skeet finished for her, "Throwing a glass at a car."

Silence lingered for a few seconds before Karen questioned, "How did you know that, Malu."

"I'm at your front door. Would you mind letting me in?" inquired Skeet.

Karen walked down the stairs slowly, hesitant to let him in. But she could not leave him on the other side of the door. This wasn't her vision of how they would meet up again. When she opened the door, Skeet stood dressed simple wearing denim jeans, white shirt, and white leather Gucci sneakers.

"Are you going to invite me in?" Skeet questioned.

Karen unlocked the screen door and let him inside.

Skeet looked around at all the boxes and various items scattered around on the floor. The notice to vacate was on full display on the coffee table. Karen was embarrassed and didn't know what to say. She stood back and burst into tears. She took a seat on one of the boxes.

Skeet walked over to her and kneeled, taking her hands away from her face and wiped her tears. "It's going to be okay, and you don't have to be embarrassed."

"I'm so sorry you had to see me like this. I just came back home, and things had fallen apart. The car I threw the glass at was my brother. He just left me in this situation," said Karen.

"How about we go get a drink, have a meal, and talk about things so we can come up with a solution." Skeet was now standing over Karen and extending his hand to her.

Karen looked up at Skeet and put her hand into his. He pulled her up from the box. She grabbed her purse and the two exited. Skeet hurried to his Jeep Rubicon and opened the passenger door. Once Karen was inside, she relaxed in the soft seat. She was grateful that Skeet had come to take her away even if it was just for a short time. Skeet took her to one of his favorite steak houses in Baton City.

Over dinner, Karen savored the succulent medium well-cooked KC Strip. Skeet offered his ear while she explained everything. As he listened, he already had a plan to solve Karen's problems. If he had his way, she would never return to the trashy place he had picked her up from. Ever since laying eyes on Karen, he wanted her and would make her his woman.

After dinner and wine, Karen was in good spirits. Skeet took care of the bill and exited the establishment, but their night was not over. They drove around downtown for a couple of hours talking and laughing while drinking and smoking weed. When it got late, Skeet took Karen to a building of apartments located in the downtown area. The two entered the elevator and road to the top floor.

When the elevator door opened, Karen almost lost her breath. She had no idea that something this nice existed in her city.

"Are you going to stay inside?" questioned Skeet, exiting the elevator.

The dim lights brightened, showing off the beautifully decorated penthouse. Karen instantly fell in love with the place, especially the view of Baton City.

"I love your place," complimented Karen, still looking around.

"This is not my place. Well, not my home. But I don't mind helping someone in need. I don't use this place often enough, so you and your mother are welcome to stay here. Your presence would make me want to be here more," said Skeet, handing Karen a joint.

Karen was in disbelief. She expected Skeet to get her intoxicated, bring her back to his house, and fuck her before dropping her back home with a doggy bag. That's what Zak always did when she was having family problems.

"Why are you doing so much for me? We just slept together," asked Karen.

Skeet looked out at the view. It was time to tell her who he was.

"You may not see it right now, but I see your potential and good heart. Please allow me to get to know you. I won't allow my daughter's best friend and my future woman to be out in the cold." Skeet waited for her reaction.

Karen stepped back almost stumbling over the glass coffee table. "Wait! Your daughter! You are Rena's father? You knew this from day one! Why didn't you tell me!" she yelled.

"If I would have told you who I was, would you have been open to get to know me?" questioned Skeet.

"Maybe! Did Rena know about this?" questioned Karen, now pacing behind the white leather couch.

"No. But can you handle this or not?" asked Skeet, now sitting at the bar.

"I am fine with things, but how would Rena feel? She just found out about you and lost someone awfully close to her. Now she must worry about her best friend in an intimate relationship with her father." Karen folded her arms and waited for Skeet to respond. The situation was complicated, but she hoped that Skeet had a remedy because she didn't want to let him go.

Skeet shook his head, stood from the bar, and walked over to her. He gently kissed her on the forehead. "The offer still stands. No matter if you want me or not, I am still helping my daughter's best friend. I want you, but I can give you your space and let you decide if you want me. There are keys to a white range rover in the garage so you can get yourself around and make some moves," said Skeet before making his way to the elevator door.

"So how would I contact you, Malu? I mean, Skeet," asked Karen.

Skeet turned around with a smile on his face. "I will be in touch with you, Karen, and I am still Malu to you."

Karen stood in the middle of the living room and watched Skeet disappear behind the elevator door.

REVEAL

Kay'Ron parked the black range rover in his driveway. He looked into the rear-view mirror at Kade who was sitting in his car seat playing with a toy.

After Shawneece's death, he was taking care of his son by himself and had not been seen much by anyone. Corrine and Alice called him daily, but he never answered. Marvin popped up from time to time, but Kay'Ron made the visits short and sweet.

He finally had some peace of mind especially after dealing with Shawneece's family. They showed up and tried to control the situation until it was time to pay for the burial. Kay'Ron stepped up and paid for everything, it was the least he could do for his son's mother. He even went as far as speaking at the funeral. But it was not enough to stop the wrath of Shawneece's family. Her half-brother James had a gun, and while Kay'Ron spoke, James disrupted everything by drawing it. Kay'Ron only spared James because his father was able to get possession of the gun and get his son out of the sanctuary.

That memory still haunted Kay'Ron's thoughts as he exited the vehicle. He retrieved his son from the back seat before going inside the house. It was Sunday and he was looking forward to making a seafood boil and watching the sports channel while Kade played with his toys.

Once inside, he noticed someone slipped a brown envelope through the mail slot. Kay'Ron found it odd because mail was never delivered on Sundays. He also noticed the envelope had no mailing stamps or return address. Before grabbing the envelope from the floor, he got Kade settled into his playpen, taking off his shoes and turning on cartoons. He went back to the envelope and stared at it for a moment before picking it up. He took a seat, opened the envelope carefully, and began reviewing the documents inside. The first document was a marriage certificate from Florida with Marvin and Shawneece's name on it.

"This is who he was married to?" Kay'Ron rambled to himself remembering the conversation he had in the past with his uncle. The second document was Marvin and Shawneece's divorce decree along with birth certificates proving that Shawneece had other children.

Infuriated, Kay'Ron grabbed Kade and put his shoes on quickly. He headed back out of the house making sure he had the documents. After securing Kade in his seat, he got in the driver's seat and backed out the driveway, almost colliding with a car that was coming down the street. While driving, he called Zak and instructed him to meet him at Corrine's before hanging up.

At Corrine's, Sarah, her daughters, Alice, and Marvin were enjoying Sunday dinner. Several minutes later, they heard Kay'Ron parking in the driveway. "Oh, looks like Kay'Ron decided to join us after all!" yelled Corrine from the kitchen.

Kay'Ron exited, grabbed Kade who was now asleep and hurried to the front door. At that moment, Zak had parked, got out and was slowly jogging, catching up with him at the door.

"Hey, cuz, what's going on? Is Corrine okay?"

Kay'Ron did not answer Zak. Once inside, he handed Kade to Alice and went to the dining room where Marvin sat at the head of Corrine's table finishing up his oxtails.

Kay'Ron slammed the envelope down on the table in front of him, causing everyone to focus their attention on the dining room. "When the fuck were you going to tell me that you and Shawneece were married!"

Stunned, Zak snatched the envelope from the table, removed the contents, and began reviewing the documents. When finished, he tossed the paperwork on the table, giving Marvin a look of contempt while speaking, "Man, you are something else. Is this one of the reasons you came back home years ago?"

Marvin ignored Zak's question and focused on Kay'Ron. "I didn't think it mattered since you were already balls deep in her."

Suddenly, Corrine came out of the kitchen and smacked Marvin across the face before addressing him, "You mean to tell me you got married and never told us!" When Marvin did not respond fast enough, she smacked him a second time. "I know what this is about! You have been mad since my sister's funeral. Boy, I tell you one thing, I could not love the envy out of you. You have been jealous of so many people for years! Your sister, my late husband, and I had no idea your own nephew. No wonder he stopped looking up to you. He could probably feel the hate and lies."

Marvin was hurt by his mother's words. He had to get the heat off him. Through tear filled eyes, he looked at Sarah. "I am not the only one lying around here."

He was about to expose the paternity test results for Christina. Sarah felt lightheaded, her heart pounded.

But before he could speak, Corrine smacked him again. "This shit is about you, don't try to pull anyone else into it! Now I know I need to question some things. Is this why you knew the details of her death? You were the first person to learn about it. I saw the police report. You have details that the cops have not revealed yet. And why wasn't Kade taken by child protection? You are the one that brought that baby to me."

Everyone stared at Marvin waiting for an answer. For him, there would be no getting around because Corrine would get the answers she needed. "Fuck it! Shawneece hurt me deeply. When I got injured and the money ran out, she dumped me and aborted our baby. I didn't know about the pregnancy until I found the abortion papers in the car she was driving. But fuck her because the woman who owns my heart lives here in

Baton City. Unfortunately her heart is occupied with someone else."

He looked over in Sarah's direction. She swallowed hard. Now that she had Kay'Ron where she wanted him, she didn't need Marvin blowing it all.

"Get to the point of the story with your victim ass!" yelled Corrine.

On the spot by everyone, Marvin had nothing to lose at this point. He decided to tell the truth. "Ever since I saw Shawneece with Kay'Ron, she has been avoiding my calls and texts. I tried to tell her to leave and never return, she laughed in my face. Then she had his son and was taunting me with that. Finally, I went to her house and made her write a suicide letter. Then I strangled the bitch with a belt and hung her in the kitchen doorway so it could look like a suicide. The cable guy was a friend of mine. I took Kade and waited for him to notify the authorities."

"Was the cable guy Carlton?" questioned Zak.

Corrine yelled, "Carlton! He popped up at the hospital when Christine was born."

Marvin's hands began to shake as he watched his family begin to piece things together. They found out about almost everything but Natty, Roxanne, and Sarah. The walls were closing in, but Marvin was too afraid to stand on his feet. He didn't know who in the room would attack first, including his mother.

As Zak observed, it was clear that Marvin's nervousness was validation that he was linked to Roxanne's attack. Now Zak just needed to figure out how to break it to Kay'Ron without losing his trust. He looked down at the envelope wondering if there was any more information that Kay'Ron may have missed. He checked inside the brown envelope and found a small white envelope.

While he opened and removed the contents, Marvin responded to his question, "No, it was my homeboy Steve." He wondered why Zak brought up Carlton. That could only mean that Zak knew about his connection to Roxanne's abduction. His mother did not make it any better mentioning Carlton's visit to the hospital.

"Hey, Kay'Ron, did you see this?" Zak handed him the two folded pieces of paper.

Everyone sat in silence as Kay'Ron read the contents of the documents, his face changed from serious to anger. It was proof that Marvin was Christina's biological father. The second paper revealed that Marvin was responsible for setting his own sister up to go to prison. Zak handed that paperwork to Corrine and shook his head exiting the dining room. Corrine looked over the paperwork and tears began running from her eyes. Her son was officially a Loyal Snake.

"You bastard, you set your sister up to go to prison!" She threw the papers on the table and hurried out of the dining room.

Kay'Ron took a seat and looked at the man that was causing all his pain. He had been punishing his mother all these years and it was not entirely her fault she was gone.

Marvin could see the hurt in his nephew's eyes. "I am sorry."

With a glazed face, Kay'Ron looked his uncle in the eyes. "I don't know how." He turned his focus to Sarah.

"Kay'Ron, I am sorry, I can explain." She took a seat at the table.

"How long?" he questioned.

"Since I was in high school, Marvin would come up to Baton City and we spent time together. During those times, he was giving me the attention I wanted from you. Things just went too far but I was waiting for you, and you never truly came back to me," said Sarah. She buried her face in her hands and cried.

Defeated, Kay'Ron spoke, "Sarah, I put you through a lot and I am sorry. You needed love that I could not give you. This shit is fucked up, but I understand that you had needs. I was fucking around with a lot of bitches and keeping you on standby. I want to say that I am sorry, and I love you because you have given me two beautiful daughters."

Corrine and Zak stood in the doorway in tears as they witnessed their family disassemble.

"Marvin, I don't know what I ever did to you. I used to think you had my back. I even looked up to you and all this time you have been a Loyal Snake. You could have had any woman, but you chose Sarah and that was only to hurt me. Now I see why you go through the shit you do."

Kay'Ron grabbed one of the glasses from the table and helped himself to some scotch. What his uncle had done to him over the years was catastrophic. If he stood up and killed him at that moment, it still would not be enough. Everyone expected him to snap, but Kay'Ron was surprised that although he was stewing with several emotions, his disposition was now humble.

Marvin grabbed his drink. When he tilted the glass to his mouth, Corrine smacked it out of his hand. "You know what, I prayed that you did not display the tendencies in your true bloodline, but you did." Everyone looked at each other in confusion as she continued, "I am not your biological mother; David is not your father. Your mother Scarlett was a good friend of mine. We grew up from childhood together. She was the biggest snake you could ever know. That woman had no loyalty to anyone. She lived a dangerous life scamming people, setting people up to die, boosting, anything she had to do to get money. She fell for your father Gregory and got pregnant with you, and I saw a different side of her. She was in love with your father and was willing to change for the family life. But your father was a homosexual and left her hanging to be with his true love in Georgia. Scarlett did not want you if she could not have Gregory. She was going to leave you on an orphanage doorstep. David was against it, but I took you in and no matter how much we tried to love you, at the end you still ended up like Scarlett."

"Where is my mother now?" questioned Marvin.

"She was murdered a year after she abandoned you," answered Corrine.

"Is my father still alive?"

Corrine tossed an envelope over to Marvin. "Far as I know he is still alive. He lives in New Orleans."

Marvin stood from the table and took the walk of shame through the dining room. When he made it to Zak, he stopped and questioned, "Why did you ask me about Carlton?"

Zak gave a wicked smile. "Because that is your do dirt buddy. Outside he was at the hospital the same day Christina died. He never came and spoke to the family, just you. That seems suspicious like maybe there are more bones that will be falling out your closet."

With no words, Marvin went out the front door. He heard the door lock quickly. He retrieved his cell from his pocket and dialed Carlton. He answered on the first ring. Marvin spoke in a whisper as he hurried to his car, "Zak is a problem. He needs to go now."

Skeet

The next day at home, Skeet sat across the table trying to enjoy his brunch. Living in a home with a Rachel who was unhappy and Janice who he wanted to kill was wretchedness.

"Damn, your maid makes one of the best mimosas that I ever had," said Janice.

It took everything in Skeet's power not to kill her in cold blood at that moment. He would execute phase two of his plan today and Borya was meeting with him for an update.

Rachel entered the kitchen not saying a word to anyone. She plopped down onto the chair and began eating her breakfast. Skeet was already on edge with Janice and the last thing he needed was to deal with Rachel's attitude. He dismissed himself from the table and was walking out when he ran into Rena.

"Oh, I see you found the book I left in your bedroom. Out of all five editions, the 3rd one is still the best. They destroyed all the copies of that edition except for that one," said Skeet, letting out a devious laugh.

"You are wrong, I have a copy also," said Borya, entering the kitchen.

Janice was rattled by both Rena and Borya's presence. Skeet observed her demeanor.

"Janice, I expected your attendance or even condolences in regard to my mother's passing," said Borya, studying her reaction.

Janice cleared her throat. She could feel her palms sweating so she sat her drink down before replying, "My apologies, I regret I missed it. I was not sure that it would be appropriate since I am merely a stranger. Will you guys excuse me, I need a bathroom break, too many mimosas." Everyone watched her exit.

"I never knew the lady either, that's why I did not go," mumbled Rachel, tossing her toast onto her plate.

"Now that's uncalled for Rachel," fired Rena, stepping closer to the table.

"Oh, I am sorry, you guys were close. You were her favorite," said Rachel, standing up and walking away.

Rena turned to Borya and Skeet, pointing to Rachel with a perplexed look on her face.

"Don't worry about that, she doesn't understand that she is poking a bear," said Skeet. He gestured for everyone to follow him to the balcony.

Once on the balcony, Borya looked around making sure Janice was not in earshot. "What's going on? You are playing house and shit."

"That's what I was thinking uncle," said Rena.

Offended, Skeet gave them both a sarcastic look. "Come on. You two should know me by now. This is a part of the plan. In fact, phase two of the plan is going into motion today, why you think she is walking around silly off mimosas." Skeet gestured for Rena and Borya to follow him to his office.

On the way, Janice came out the bathroom almost running into Skeet. "Damn, are you okay? Maybe you should go lay down for a bit," said Skeet.

"It's the mimosas," responded Janice.

"I will come check on you after I meet with Rena and Borya about her next trip," instructed Skeet.

Everyone walked past Janice leaving her in the hallway. When they were out of sight, she went to Skeet's bedroom to lay down.

Inside the office, Borya wasted no time. "I have the footage from the inside of the boutique with me." He handed Skeet a small camera device. "Mother had a hidden video camera. It was damaged bad during the fire, but my guy was able to salvage it."

Skeet looked over at Rena. "I need your head in this. You remember chapter one in Soring Eagle? You can't allow your emotions to dictate your moves. What you are about to see will be emotional for you and I need you to not react."

"I have not even seen it yet myself or I would have been here sooner," said Borya, wiping sweat from his forehead before taking a drink of scotch.

They hovered around the desk and watched the recording of Janice murder Lada in cold blood. The audio footage revealed the reason why.

When the video ended, everyone sat in silence for several minutes before Borya spoke, "So, this cunt was Daubs ex-girlfriend's daughter."

Rena continued to sit in silence indignant. Her father shared the same emotions. It was difficult to keep himself tamed and follow the same advice he had given his daughter. Once again, someone had hurt a woman in his life.

"Trust me, I got this. It will take patience and you two will witness things but remember it will all be a part of the plan. I am my father's son on this one. My plan will take months to fulfill, and she will be a part of the household from this day moving forward. Remember chapter two in Soring Eagle."

"Keep your enemy exceptionally close. Like a snake and its owner. Take the time to size him up, then eat him," both Borya and Rena finished his words in unison.

Changing the subject, "Rena, how was your sleep in your brand-new loft downtown?" questioned Borya.

"Oh, it's beautiful, but I still wish I had the penthouse dad showed me first with the private pool."

"Well, honey, that one is in use at the moment," responded Skeet, thinking about Karen.

"Don't worry, you are not going to spend much time in your loft," said Borya, handing her the folder.

When she opened the folder, it was an acceptance letter to the Soring Eagle retreat. "Omg, yes! I have been waiting for a response. I didn't think I would get in because I had to take leave."

"Your grandfather is now one of the founders, so you got pull," answered Skeet.

"This place is essential to your skills as an assassin. The top assassins in the world trained here, including Bly, who is now one of the instructors," said Borya, giving her a wink.

"So, when do I leave?" questioned Rena.

Borya and Skeet looked at each other with a sly look and responded in unison, "Tomorrow evening."

This was perfect, Rena thought. She needed a distraction because she was tempted to go find Kay'Ron. "Okay, I am going to check on Karen and spend some time with her before I leave." Rena exited the office.

"She is going to be one of the best. I can see it," said Borya.

"Definitely, as much as I want her not to be, she will be," responded Skeet.

Borya inquired, "You know, I was going to wait, but I must know, what is the plan? You said this woman will be staying on your estate for a few months. What old Daubs tactic do you have?"

Skeet answered before lighting a cigar, "She took one life from me, so she owes me one. It must be just as meaningful as my mother. Just think of the moment a woman lays eyes on their child. They fall into a deep love for them. I want her to feel that tender love before taking her away from it."

"Let me get this straight, you are going to get her pregnant then kill her after she gives birth? Damn, you are your father's son," said Borya.

Skeet saw Borya out the mansion and returned to the family room where Janice was relaxing watching television. "I thought I told you to wait for me in the bedroom," flirted Skeet.

He was highly attracted to her beauty since the day she approached him at the cemetery. He had plans to finish his final years with her. But that was all tarnished and she had to go. He wrapped his arms around Janice from the back and began planting soft kisses on her neck. When she stood up, he guided her around the couch to him and pressed himself on her so she could feel his manhood growing. His touch was what Janice had been yearning for. He led her up the stairs and down the long hall to his suite on the north side of the mansion.

Once inside the suite, Janice turned, now facing him. She met his lips and slid her soft tongue into his mouth. They kissed passionately while Skeet guided her to the bed. There would be no fourplay because that was for people in love. He slipped her jeans down to her knees and ripped her panties just enough to enter.

Skeet filled her up deep and wide. Damn she felt tight, warm, wet. Janice winced when he began pounding her pussy. Her juices welcomed him with every thrust. He almost got lost and had to refocus, reminding himself that this ecstasy would have an expiration date. He burst inside of her and leaned in, making sure all his juice spilled into her. It had been less than ten minutes, but Janice laid sprawled out on the bed like he fucked her for hours. Skeet went to the bathroom to clean up. While showering, Janice joined. He wasn't getting off that easy. She dropped to her knees and wrapped her warm mouth around him, bringing it back to attention.

"Ready for round two?" whispered Skeet in a seductive voice. He grabbed her by her hair, pulling her up to meet his face. He turned her around aggressively, not wanting her to see the malice in his eyes and entered her from the back. He whispered, "Are you ready to carry my son?"

"Yes, I am ready to do whatever you want me to do," whispered Janice, anticipating him entering her again.

This time, Skeet dug deep into her walls trying to punish her. Her pussy was good, and he was trying not to succumb to it. Janice liked the rough sex. If he continued fucking her like this, she was not going anywhere.

"Skeet, I love you!" Her tone was sensual, making him go harder. If only this bitch did not kill his mother. "Give it all to me, hurt me, do what you want, I need to have your baby," whined Janice.

Skeet released inside her, barely able to keep his balance. They showered and Janice returned to his bed and went straight to sleep. Skeet stayed in the bathroom looking in the mirror. Step one of his plan was in motion. When he exited the bathroom, Janice was already snoring in bed. Skeet dressed and went to his office to handle a couple things before going downtown to visit Karen.

Once Rena was back in the city, she dialed Karen's number. The phone rang once before Karen answered, "Damn, Rena, what the hell? I have been trying to contact you for days!"

"I apologize, I just been dealing with a lot of stuff. Are you at one of the spots?" said Rena.

"No, I have been avoiding the spot since we touched down. Just not feeling like arguing with Zak," replied Karen.

"Girl, where are you? I will come to you," asked Rena. Karen gave Rena the address and she entered it into her GPS.

Ten minutes later, she was in front of a familiar building. She parked and went inside to the elevators in the lobby. When she got on the elevator, she pressed P. If she recalled, this was the building her father took her to months back. When the elevator opened, it was confirmed. It was the place and Karen was standing right in it.

"Wow, this is the place my father owns," said Rena, exiting the elevator.

Instead of answering, Karen handed Rena a photo of Skeet. "Malu, the mystery man in Russia is Skeet, your father. I just found out when we returned," said Karen in a low voice, not knowing what reaction to expect from her friend.

Rena remembered Skeet offering to keep Karen company while she went on the job with Borya. Then he made sure Rena didn't return right after the hit. Karen never contacted Rena at all during her trip, and finally Skeet never showed his face in the same room when she and Karen where together, not even at Lada's funeral.

"Wow, so you're going to be my stepmom bestie," said Rena, flopping down on the couch.

She was taking lives these days and did not have any room to judge. The relationship between Karen and her father would just make it official that Karen was family without a doubt. In addition, it was an upgrade from Zak's no-good ass.

Karen sighed in relief. "Girl, I thought you were going to be mad as hell at me."

Rena gave her a sarcastic look. "You had no control over what happened. When I think back, it's obvious that Skeet was intentionally keeping us from finding out."

They laughed at the situation. Then Karen explained how she ended up in the penthouse. After conversating for an hour, they headed to the mental health facility to check on Karen's mother. She was under a thirty-day observation.

On the way it began to storm. The raindrops tapping the window was tranquilizing to Rena as she rode. Karen's phone rang, she looked, and it was Zak. She gripped the steering wheel and shook her head. Rena did not have to look over at her to know who was calling.

"Karen, my father goes for what he wants and if you are not sure, please keep it real with him," she warned.

"Don't worry, I will handle his heart carefully. He knows everything, even the stuff I have not told him. You know, this feels like a dream."

"Welcome to my world, you are going to be pinching yourself a lot," said Rena.

Karen parked in the parking lot of the mental health facility. The rain was pouring so they decided to wait for it to slow down so they could go inside.

Karen looked over at Rena. "Are you okay? I know you two did not go that hard for each other only to just stop feeling anything. Trust me, I know."

Rena gazed at the heavy rain beating down the window. Karen was right, she had suppressed emotions that needed to be resolved. She needed to embrace the hurt she was feeling so that she could forgive Kay'Ron and free her heart to love someone else.

"I loved him and thought we were going to be together forever." Rena allowed the tears to stream from her eyes.

"I know how you feel. It was your first love, and he will always be in your heart. Trust me, I don't think he had intended things to go south like this. He just has a lot of things going on in his life that he never resolves so it just keeps coming back. I also think that he was still grieving the loss of Roxanne and you were like a breath of fresh air for him. You're young and you are off to bigger and better things. So please forgive him and set yourself free so you can grow," advised Karen.

Suddenly, the rain stopped, the clouds parted, and the sun was beaming. Rena wiped her tears, turned to Karen, and smiled. She was right, it was okay to love Kay'Ron. But it was time to forgive him and let him go because she had so much more to live for. They exited the car and hurried inside to visit Karen's mother.

GOODBYE BATON CITY

"You're sure you want to take the bus?" questioned Daubs.

Kay'Ron assured Daubs that he was fine and would contact him when he arrived at his destination.

Sandy made a final attempt to reach out to Kay'Ron and insisted that he come to California because it was urgent. After finding out all the things Marvin had done, Kay'Ron decided that he and Kade needed to get away from Baton City so he could clear his mind and find peace. Words could not explain how hurt and confused he felt. A man who was not even family had sabotaged every stride he tried to make. With no one to trust, he reached out to Daubs and when he made it home that night, he was waiting for him.

Kay'Ron explained everything that went down. Daubs used his connections to facilitate a video chat with his mother.

When Natty assured Kay'Ron that Daubs had his back, he decided to leave his business affairs to Daubs while he was away. He was not sure how long he would be gone. If the move became permanent, he would arrange for his daughters to come whenever they wanted.

"Yeah, Kade and I will enjoy the ride. It will give me time to think and clear my head before seeing Sandy," said Kay'Ron.

"I totally get it. Don't worry, I will contact you the moment I get Natty out," said Daubs. He handed Kay'Ron an envelope. "Make sure you read this letter preferably while you are taking this bus ride. It's from your mother. She decided it was time for her to clear the air with you as well. Trust me, what she must tell you is not half as bad as what Marvin has created in your life."

When the woman spoke over the intercom, Kay'Ron grabbed the envelope, folded it, and put it inside his back pocket. He took Kade from Daubs and walked over to the bus driver who was instructing everyone to load their bags. Daubs watched Kay'Ron get onto the bus and take his seat.

As the bus drove away, Daubs felt sad. He was growing fond of Kay'Ron and looked at him as a son. When he learned that his granddaughter Rena was having an affair with Kay'Ron, Daubs had to guide him to Roxanne to protect his granddaughter. He had witnessed the love he shared with Roxanne and if she was alive, Kay'Ron would never love another woman.

For the next twenty-four hours Kay'Ron and Kade enjoyed their trip. They took pictures at every stop. When they arrived at the bus terminal in San Diego, Lenny was waiting by his car. Kay'Ron stepped off the bus, grabbed his bag, and walked over to Lenny.

"Man, you still have this car," Kay'Ron joked, greeting Lenny with a hug.

While Kay'Ron secured Kade in the car seat, Lenny tossed the duffle bag in the trunk and got inside the driver seat. He waited for Kay'Ron to get settled into the passenger seat before answering, "You damn right. Brought Sandy down here in it and it's still in the best shape. I could have drove it to Baton City to pick you up."

They both laughed. Lenny started the car and drove away. While heading to Sandy's, Kay'Ron brought Lenny up to speed on everything. When they arrived, Kay'Ron got Kade out of the car as Lenny grabbed the bag. He looked around, relieved to see something different other than the depressing Baton City streets. At that moment, he realized he had not left Baton City since his last trip with Roxanne. It was only to St. Louis, Missouri, but he remembered how much fun they had together couped up in the lavish hotel.

"Let me take Kade and you take this heavy bag. I am sure you are going to need your arms free when the door opens," said Lenny.

Kay'Ron handed over his son and took the bag before following Lenny.

When they arrived at the front door, Lenny unlocked the door before stepping to the side allowing Kay'Ron in first.

Sandy was much healthier after completing her treatments. She held David and hurried over to Kay'Ron, who kneeled and allowed her to kiss him on the cheek. "I'm so happy to see you," said Sandy.

Kay'Ron looked at the toddler she was holding. "Damn, you and Lenny had a child? No wonder you needed me to come down because I would not have believed this information over the phone."

"Oh no, honey, this is my grandson David," answered Sandy.

She waited for Kay'Ron to respond but instead there was a perplexed look on his face. Roxanne never told him about any siblings. Before he could say anything, he heard a familiar voice say his name. He turned around and Roxanne was standing there. He stood frozen for several seconds wondering if he was hallucinating again.

"Kay'Ron, Roxanne lives," whispered Sandy.

Kay'Ron walked over to her slowly in disbelief. It was when he caught wind of her favorite shampoo that he dropped to his knees and wrapped his arms around Roxanne's waist. He began crying tears of serenity, not caring about his masculinity.

After all the pain he went through, the woman he truly loved was still in the universe with him. Now the image of the lifeless body in the trunk of the car and again on the slab at the mortuary would no longer haunt his thoughts. The warmth of her body serenaded his soul, he didn't want to let her go. Sandy brought David over and handed him over to Roxanne who kneeled down to meet Kay'Ron's face. At that moment, just looking in her eyes seemed to bring back all their memories.

"We survived the attack. This is your son David. I tried to wait patiently for this moment, but Zak was taking so long, I had to take matters in my own hands," said Roxanne.

Kay'Ron invited his firstborn son into his arms as he continued to cry.

Just as fast as things fell apart, it all began coming back together for him. He spent years fighting to get his family out of the hood. He lost people who were the truest to him. He learned his circle was broken and he could not trust the people he was giving his loyalty to.

For years, Kay'Ron struggled to regain his happiness, but it was just one disappointment after another. He now understood that the universe had broken him down so that he could learn from his mistakes and receive his blessings. He reunited with the love of his life and his mother would be home soon. And most of all, his firstborn son was alive. A foundation built on pain and lies would have to crumble so you can rebuild. Kay'Ron was at ground zero and ready to take the right path. His next chapter would be filled with peace, love, and happiness. Goodbye Baton City.

At home, Rena lounged in her bed staring out at the wonderful view of downtown Baton City. She was thinking about the latest gossip from Karen about Kay'Ron finding out what his uncle Marvin was doing. She felt bad for him and tried to reach out, but his phone number was disconnected. She asked Karen to see about getting his number from Zak who refused because he despised Rena. Maybe it was for the best, Rena thought to herself. Her daydreaming was interrupted when her cell vibrated, it was her uncle. She picked it up and answered.

"Rena, I was reviewing your transcript and another independent kill can get you a lot of points. Let me know if you need any leads and I can put you on a kill while you are in the city," said Borya.

"Thanks, unc, but the assignment specified that I had to find my own kill. I want to prove myself to everyone. They already think I am getting help because my family owns the school," responded Rena.

"Very good, talk to you soon then. I want all the details once you complete this task, because afterwards you will qualify for independent contracts and that's where you start making your own money," said Borya before ending the call.

Rena tossed the phone beside her and continued her gaze out the floor to ceiling windows. She already had her kill set up thanks to an anonymous source that provided evidence that Shawneece and Shavon were the cause of her miscarriage. Since Shawneece was already dead, Rena could only get Shavon. She took one week leave from Soring Eagle to execute the kill. She hoped to find out the men involved to get full vengeance because a double or triple kill would get her fifty plus points, making her eligible for the Rhodium tag achievement. If she had that metal, she would be in high demand for contracts. The only person who had that tag was her grandfather. No one had been able to achieve the Rhodium, but she was close.

Her plan was to complete the kill at nightfall. She knew Shavon had been at Kay'Ron's spot living it up like it was her place. Taking advantage of the fact Kay'Ron was MIA and Zak was preoccupied with getting Karen back under his thumb. She hated that Zak was still able to hold her friend emotionally hostage, but Karen was staying transparent with her father, so she chose to stay out of it.

When night fell, Rena headed over to the spot. She drove past, confirming that neither Kay'Ron nor Zak was there. The dim light and two shadows in the picture window indicated

Shavon was not alone. Rena parked the black van in the alley and exited, walking half a block to the back of the spot.

She wore an all-black jumpsuit and kept her cap low to conceal her face. All she needed was her trusty nine-millimeter and forty-five. She knew Kay'Ron always kept gasoline in the storage room for his four wheelers. When she was done, she would burn the place up. A fire was an extra point on the assignment.

When she entered the back yard, she noticed the kitchen window was open. She eased to get a peek inside, hearing male and female voices. The smell of PCP lingered out the window.

"So, when you going to get that nigga here?" questioned Shawneece's brother James before taking another shot of the whisky.

"I tried to call him, and his phone is disconnected. But he never goes a week without stopping by here. Plus, his dog is still here, and he doesn't play about him," responded Shavon.

"Shit, I really need to know where that nigga lay his head," said James.

"Well, I don't know all that, he has several places he stays, and you just never know his moves. Zak would probably come through. They are so unpredictable," replied Shavon.

"Don't worry, I have a plan for the unexpected. If that nigga Zak pops up, I will hold him hostage until Kay'Ron comes," spoke James.

"Just in time and two for the price of one," whispered Rena with a smile. She was going to get those points.

Karma is best served cold. People do grimy shit then relax as if it all goes away. This is how we get caught, forgetting that we violated someone, not doing our homework on how dangerous our opponents are.

Rena screwed the silencer onto her gun and crept around to the side door. The lock was messed up, but no one knew about it but she and Kay'Ron. He told her about the door for emergency purposes. It led straight to his basement bedroom. She remembered spending a couple nights there when Kay'Ron was handling business. Rena crept inside, eased through the dark room and up the stairs, stopping at the door to listen.

"While we wait, let me take some steam off of you," said Shavon, now high and horny.

James gave a devious smile. He got a rush thinking about fucking Kay'Ron's hoe in his bed before killing him. The PCP had him feeling like he was floating on air. Shavon grabbed his hand and led him to the bedroom. As he followed her down the hall, his dick rose for the occasion as he watched her juicy ass wiggle through the leggings, she wore no panties.

While they were headed to the bedroom, Rena was in the front of the house dousing it with gasoline, making sure to give them time to get into their flow.

"Stay right here, Buck," Rena ordered before making her way to the bedroom.

Ten minutes passed, and she was ready to crash their party. She did not know anything about James, so she assumed he was experienced. When she heard moaning, she stepped inside the bedroom where Shavon was riding James. Rena had to admit the girl had skills, but her pussy had a horrible stench lingering around the room. She stood for a couple minutes allowing James and Shavon to get their rocks off.

"Damn, baby, your pussy good. But you need to go see a doctor about BV," said James with his eyes still closed.

Rena walked up to the bed unnoticed and aimed the gun to the back of Shavon head. "You right about that. Bitch, your pussy stank." Both Shavon and James opened their eyes and focused on Rena.

"What the fuck!" yelled Shavon. She sat down next to James.

"Who the fuck is this bitch?" questioned James.

He was not moved by the female standing over him with a gun. Rena had no time to introduce herself to James, so she pulled the trigger and put a bullet in his head then pointed the gun at Shavon.

"Please don't kill me. I can tell you who is behind Roxanne's death," pleaded Shavon.

"Get to talking!" demanded Rena, playing along.

"Marvin called it. He was jealous of Roxanne's success. He will kill you if you get in the way of his plan to get back on top," said Shavon, now crying.

Rena smirked. "I doubt it but thanks for the information. And what about what you did?" Rena smacked her with the gun.

Wincing in pain, Shavon struggled to speak, "I am sorry. Sarah and Shawneece set it up. They were afraid you were going to take over like Roxanne especially when they found out you was pregnant."

Rena fired the gun twice killing Shavon. She exited the bedroom. Once in the living room, she instructed Buck to follow her out the back door. She tossed a lit match inside the open window initiating the flames. For the next half hour, she and Buck sat in the van and watched the Norton spot burn. She checked Karen's phone location and rolled her eyes noticing she was at the white house. She headed over there to leave Buck with Zak.

She parked out front and walked up to the door with Buck following behind. She knocked twice. Zak flung the door open agitated. "Kay'Ron is not here. How did you know about this place."

"I know everything," answered Rena.

Karen came to the door and stood next to Zak with a worried expression on her face. "You good, Karen?" questioned Rena.

Karen nodded, closing her shirt.

Rena returned her gaze to Zak. "The Norton spot is burned to the ground and there are two bodies in it. I killed Shavon because she was the reason why I was attacked. A man named James was there also, he was planning to kill you and Kay'Ron. Shavon told me that Sarah also took part in the attack against me, and Marvin was the mastermind behind Roxanne's murder."

Zak's agitated expression changed to shock. All the pieces of the puzzle were solved. Marvin still had a secret to take to the grave and so did Sarah. "Rena, I am sorry for treating you so badly. Thank you, I hope we can move forward and have better days and help each other. I know you taste Sarah's blood. But can you do me a favor and let me holla at Kay'Ron about her. He needs to decide on what to do with her," Zak said.

Rena turned and walked away. She wasn't accepting any apologies or making any promises. She would go back to

Soring Eagle and finish with honors. That was all the time Zak

and Kay'Ron would have to deal with Sarah before she did.

RHODIUM TAG

Two months went by, and Rena finished the year at the top of her class. She was the second assassin in history to receive the Rhodium tag. Daubs was a proud man.

To celebrate, Rena and Bly arrived in Baton City so that Rena could visit family before returning to Soring Eagle for her final year. She showed him around her city, and they enjoyed dinner with Skeet, Daubs, Janice, Sanity, Donavan, Lydia, and Rachel before returning to her loft.

"This city life is cool. It's been so long since I experienced it. I could get used to this," said Bly, enjoying his cigar and the beautiful night view.

Rena sat next to him with her leg on his enjoying her wine. The city had transformed over the years, no longer looking like a country town. Now Baton City was almost equivalent to going to New York City, Los Angeles, Atlanta, or Miami. The entertainment district took the credit for the upgrade of the city.

"Having this place to come to is great. I am glad I did not give it up," said Rena.

Bly was her man now and she was happy. He poured into her never missing a beat. He treated her like a queen and Rena was soaring around at her highest vibration. When Skeet observed his daughter's transformation, he knew he found the right man for her. At the beginning, he was nervous because his daughter who seemed to be infatuated with Kay'Ron, who in Skeet's eyes was not good enough.

But he knew a heavy heart could not be convinced so he stayed patient. He was ecstatic when Rena's interest peeked for Bly. Their common bond was being assassins so they would spend a lot of time together. Bly treated her like a queen and was not the type of man that fell weak to the flesh. He was damn near perfect in Skeet's eyes.

"Rena, I love you and I would come back here if that meant spending the rest of my life with you," said Bly, using one hand to rub her leg.

"I love you. I am sorry I could not deal with Australia and its natural elements. But what about your family? I don't want to be an inconvenience," responded Rena, now focusing on him.

"Honestly, they hate Australia. They have been trying to convince me to bring them back here. They want to live in Las Vegas," answered Bly.

They shared a laugh before going in for a kiss. Every time they kissed Rena felt a charge. Bly was so loving and gentle compared to the killer she witnessed on jobs. She loved how he adapted to everything. Being with him was easy and joyful even when times were challenging. They were an item and could not stand to be separated from each other for too long. Their energy vibrated for each other effortlessly. Bly willing to move back was big for her. He was showing her one of the most important things in love and that was sacrifice.

Still kissing, Bly lifted Rena and carried her to the bedroom laying her down. He loved every part of her. Her smooth skin, scent, and how vulnerable she allowed herself to be with him. Craving her juice, he used his head to open her thighs. He began massaging her clitoris gently in a circle motion with his tongue. When it swelled, he sucked gently because he loved to taste her first orgasm. Within a couple of minutes, Rena was bucking, and she released. Satisfied, Bly continued ravishing her pussy.

His dick was hard as a rock trying to break through his sweats. He wanted to feel her but loved edging himself as precum oozed from him. Building the anticipation for the grand finale, his rule was Rena had to cum three times before he went in for his. It didn't take long to reach his goal, it never did. The anticipation in his sweats had built to full compacity, he needed to dive into her ocean and stroke her walls. At his limit, he lifted his head from between her warm thick thighs and hovered over her, removing his sweats. The sight of his chocolate pole made Rena's mouth water. She sat up to taste him, but Bly stopped her.

"No, I want that tsunami I started down there," said Bly, his look both lustful and wicked.

Without warning, he flipped her over and spread her chocolate cheeks. He relished the visual of her juiciness before going in. The pussy seemed to grab him as he began to stroke. They both moaned in ecstasy. Bly was precise with his dick game. Damn, did Soring Eagle train this nigga to fuck too? Rena thought. She took every inch of him. Her hissing sound let him know she had reached another peak. Bly didn't need an hour tonight as he released his seeds inside of her. He collapsed onto the bed and scooped Rena into his arms.

They laid in silence holding each other until they fell into a deep sleep.

In the penthouse, Karen sat on the floor in the master bathroom looking at the positive pregnancy test.

"Fuck, I don't want to be a mother right now," said Karen as she tried to gather her mind to figure out a plan of action.

She knew that Skeet was not the father of the baby because they had not been active since he told her he had a baby on the way. Despite her being mad at him, that did not stop Skeet from paying the bills and placing money in a private account he set up to help her out. Karen knew the baby belonged to Zak. All these years they never slipped up; it was clear he had trapped her. She was giving him a run for his money because she did not need him financially, so Zak had to find a way to control her life and that was to get her pregnant.

She picked up her cell phone and dial Zak. He answered on the first ring.

Not giving him a chance to say hello, she began speaking, "We need to talk."

"Okay, I will be back in the city soon then we can talk," responded Zak before quickly ending the call.

Karen looked at the phone for a moment before tossing it. Feeling sick, she hovered over the toilet just in time for the vomit to shoot out of her mouth.

"Are you okay, baby?" yelled Karen's mother from the other side of the bathroom door.

"Yes, mother," she answered, laying back on the cool bathroom floor.

She hoped that her pregnancy would not be the breaking point for her and Skeet because she needed him.

In California, Roxanne and Kay'Ron relaxed on the beach. Sandy and Lenny were watching the boys to give them some alone time. The past few months had been a lot handling the boys, planning their wedding, and finding space that would accommodate their boys and Kay'Ron's daughters. Roxanne was also pregnant again so Kay'Ron found a beach home on the same strip as Sandy so that he and Roxanne could have their space but also be close. Things were going great, but Kay'Ron still had not communicated with anyone in Baton City but Daubs.

Now that Roxanne had all her memories back, they could discuss what to do with Natty's and decide if they ever wanted to go back to Baton City. Roxanne would have to continue her new alias since she was presumed deceased. Kay'Ron was proud of her because despite what happened, once she regained her memory, she had not missed a beat.

"I think we should keep Natty's and the building next door because of the location, it's going to always make a lot of money. When your mother comes home, we can give it to her as a starter gift. Your investments have been doing well and we can find other projects," said Roxanne.

"I like that idea. Have you thought about what you wanted to do after you have the baby?" questioned Kay'Ron.

"I am not sure, but my artwork has been doing well online. I want to consider purchasing a building to display and sale my work. We can get a building with multiple spaces and rent the other spaces out to creative businesses. That investment Daubs put me on scored me a lot of money, so I can buy the building straight out," said Roxanne.

"It's whatever you want to do, baby, I just love seeing you happy and achieving your dreams," said Kay'Ron.

Roxanne kissed him on the lips. Kay'Ron was a different man now and she loved the changes he made. He was attentive to her and humble.

"Kay'Ron, you have always survived, but tell me what is your dream? You never talked about anything but making money to help everyone survive. Now that we have money, what is it that you want to do with it?" queried Roxanne.

Kay'Ron sat looking at the ocean. He never thought about what his passion was. Did he even have one was the question burning in his mind. He looked at Roxanne and said, "Baby, I don't know. The goal was to make money by any means, now we are here, and I just don't know." This made him feel upset.

He looked down at the sand, but Roxanne lifted his face, looking him in his eyes. "Don't feel bad, you have a passion. It's just buried. You have been surviving all these years and suppressing yourself. Just wait and see."

"That's why I love you so much. You always see through me and find all the good I don't see. When you were gone, I didn't know what my life was supposed to be. I was just existing and trying to find comfort. With you around, I can breathe because I know you are watching when I am not," said Kay'Ron.

Roxanne kissed him again before laying her head on his shoulder. They both continued to relax for the remainder of the evening, enjoying the sunset. No kids, no worries, just love and peace of mind.

SEE NO EVIL, HEAR NO EVIL, SPEAK NO EVIL

After giving birth to their son Abriel, Janice had become comfortable flaunting around the mansion. The baby was only a month old, but she was already planning for her second pregnancy. A week prior, she overheard Skeet talking to Donavan about a surprise wedding proposal. It had to be her because far as she knew, Donavan was already married.

While Skeet was napping in the den, she ventured into his office and began rambling through the draws in hopes to come across the ring and to find where Daubs laid his head so she could have him killed. Outside the office, Rachel heard a noise and assumed it was her father. However, he was never that noisy, so she went to the door to go inside. She stopped when she saw Janice rambling. She knew her father's office was off limits unless instructed to go inside or if he was there, so she found him on the couch snoring and woke him up.

Skeet instructed Rachel to go to her suite before going to his office. He entered unnoticed and observed Janice at his desk, now trying to hack into his computer.

"Daubs," she whispered.

"What about my father?" questioned Skeet as he entered the office.

Janice jumped at the sound of his voice. She began moving slowly from behind the desk. Skeet's plan was to kill Janice at another location, but now he could not risk her getting away.

He eased towards her. "I said, why are you rambling at my desk?" He continued to close the gap between them. Janice observed the menacing look on his face. The only time she saw that look was when he killed Rachel's boyfriend.

"Why did you kill my mother?" Skeet questioned, now hovering over her like a lion stalking his prey.

"How long have you known I killed Lada?" questioned Janice. She knew she was going to die so it was no point in pleading.

"Since before we conceived Abriel," responded Skeet.

Now more angry than afraid, Janice cradled her head in both hands and began crying. She got sloppy and allowed her emotions to blind her judgement. To think that a man like Skeet would not find out she killed his mother. She should have stuck with the plan to kill everyone.

"So, this is what I get. You make me carry your son and think we are going to live happily ever after. But the reality is that you need a life for the life I took from you!" Janice yelled.

"Damn, if I didn't know any better, I would say you were a student at Soring Eagle," said Skeet.

Desperate, Janice continued, "I deserve a happy ending! Your father took my mother, then your mother took my brother. You owe me."

"Come on, do you really think that shit makes sense? You and Yasmine arranged for Rena to be kidnapped and Kyle was holding her prisoner. You were planning to kill my father. Honestly, I wanted to see you attempt that. Then you walk around here giving Rachel information about her mother's whereabout so that she can leave. You fucked up, Janice, I know everything," said Skeet in a calm voice.

"What about Abriel? He still needs me! This is what you do. Murder your children's mothers so you can possess the power over them." Janice knew those words would hurt him.

Skeet wrapped his hands around her neck and began strangling her. He looked in her eyes watching the life drain from her. It felt so good, his dick was rock hard. When her body became limp, he released his grip allowing her body to drop to the floor. He casually went over to the bar and made a drink before sitting on the sofa. He sipped his scotch while gazing at Janice's lifeless body in front of the fireplace.

In the doorway, Rachel witnessed everything. She hurried to her suite and closed the door. She retrieved a box from her vanity and put two lines of cocaine on a compact mirror. She took both lines in and stared at herself in the mirror until it began to take effect. Feeling hot, she went onto the balcony and stared off into the darkness. Janice had given her information on her mother's whereabouts.

In the office, Skeet continued to sit on the couch. He took out his cell and dialed Borya.

Skeet spoke, "Hey, brother, I need a cleanup crew, it's over."

Zak and Karen

Outside of Baton City, Zak was at his new lake house chilling with Karen. She was at the end of her 2nd trimester of pregnancy. He was lying low ever since learning about Marvin's involvement in Roxanne's attack. He made several attempts to contact Kay'Ron but had no luck. When he called Lenny, he lied to Zak like Kay'Ron instructed.

Since Karen was having his baby girl, he would put her up in the lake house to isolate her from everyone. But Karen declined. She learned how to play hardball with him. All he could do at this point was take care of his baby when she arrived. After giving birth, they would co-parent, and she would live happy ever after with Skeet.

"Are you sure you don't want to know the gender of the baby?" questioned Karen, joining Zak on the couch.

"I am sure, I want to be surprised," responded Zak, putting his arm around her.

His touch made her cringe. Karen could not wait to have this baby and resume her life with Skeet. Since Zak was getting on her nerves, she figured she would stir the pot.

"Are you going to tell your wife about the new baby?"

Her question made Zak tense up. He knew it would crush his wife to find out that he was still cheating. A new baby could be the end of their marriage and he didn't want to let her go. Yet, he wanted his children and god sister to know their sibling.

"I will tell her. I am just worried about my marriage," answered Zak.

"Wow, finally honesty. Zak, if you were worried about your marriage then you would not cheat," Karen fired back.

"Look, don't start an argument with me. We don't want to stress the baby."

They were so distracted by their conversation they did not notice Carlton standing behind them.

"I can't wait to have this baby so I can move on, and we can co-parent," said Karen, getting up from the couch.

She was going to prepare her bag and have Zak take her back to the city. When she saw Carlton standing behind the couch, she pointed while screaming. Zak turned around and stared down the barrel of Carlton's forty-five.

"You need to stay out of grown folks' business," spoke Carlton.

He pulled the trigger twice shooting Zak. He fell back off the couch onto the white rug. Carlton pointed the gun at Karen. She was still screaming, and he shot her in the head. He rummaged through the lake house, taking all the available cash before leaving their bodies to be discovered.

At the hotel, Marvin laid back in bed looking up at Sarah while she rode him.

"Fuck yeah, ride this dick, baby," he whispered. When his phone vibrated, he picked it up from his chest and read the message from Carlton: "It's done."

He smiled and tossed the phone alongside him before flipping Sarah over onto her back. He began long stroking her so good, Sarah submitted to him moaning. She hated Marvin but had to admit he had skills in the bedroom. Kay'Ron was nowhere to be found but she knew he would never be with her again. Once again, Marvin had become her support system and she was going to make the best of it. When he was about cum, she pulled him into her.

If you can't beat them then join them.

ANGEL OF DARKNESS

When Silvia arrived at the loft in Atlanta, everyone was gone. She rummaged through Donavan's desk only finding outdated bills and receipts. The refrigerator was empty, the beds were stripped, and the toys were gone. Silvia checked the alarm history to find out when the alarm was last set and it dated back over seven months ago.

"Why would he not inform me they were moving?" Silvia talked to herself as she dialed Donavan's number only to receive an error message.

She dialed Sanity's number, and she answered on the first ring, "Silvia, where the hell have you been!"

"I told you I had to get myself together. I also found my biological sister, but I have not been able to catch up with her. She resigned from her job a few months back."

"Oh yeah, what's her name?" questioned Sanity.

Silvia responded, "Lydia."

Sanity gulped her glass of champagne down while looking over at Lydia who was dancing with Donavan. "This should be interesting," she mumbled to herself.

Her brothers' love lives were always so messy.

"Where the fuck are my husband and kids?" questioned Silvia.

"Silvia, a lot has happened since you have been MIA. I have tried to contact you to make sure you were okay. And I see you have not been answering Donavan's calls either."

Silvia clinched her teeth and spoke, "What's going on, Sanity?"

Sanity gave Donavan the eye before refilling her glass. He stopped dancing and passed Lydia to his father before hurrying over to the table. He gestured for Sanity to follow him out the banquet hall into the garden out back.

Sanity put the phone on the speaker. "Like I said before, sis, I tried to contact you. Donavan moved on. He was able to divorce you and get sole custody of the children because you basically abandoned them. He is now engaged and has a daughter on the way. I am so sorry."

Silvia questioned again, "Where is my husband and my children?"

"Sorry, I can't tell you myself, but I am sure he would not be hard to find," answered Sanity.

Silvia sat on the phone in silence for several minutes. It felt like the room was spinning. Here she was off trying to get herself together. She had done everything her husband asked her to do. All she needed was a moment to find herself and she was ready to reunite with her family. Men could walk out whenever they wanted and get themselves together. But when women walked away the world turns upside down and they pay major consequences. To hear that Donavan divorced her and had another child on the way was a double smack to the face.

"Are you okay? Is there anything I can do for you?" questioned Sanity.

Instead of responding, Silvia ended the call and threw the phone across the room, shattering it against the concrete wall. She sat on the couch in the living room in the dark crying for the next hour. The love of her life left her and took her children. She wanted to kill him, but she loved him way too much to follow through and she did not want to deal with Daubs's rapture.

She had to see the woman that was enchanting her ex-husband. She wondered where he would go because he was particular about where he was rooted. She thought about all the properties they owned in the country but knew he would not dare move his new woman in a house he and her marked. The only place Silvia refused to go was Baton City. She remembered Donavan purchasing a property there. She retrieved her back up phone and dialed one of her private pilots to check for availability. Luckily, one was available to fly out within the next hour. While the pilot prepared the plane, Silvia called a cab for a ride to the airport. Donavan was not just going to toss her to the side and take her motherhood away.

At Skeet's, Sanity continued to drink from the bottle of champagne while Donavan enjoyed his cigar. On the outside, he seemed to have no worries but deep down he was nervous about the day Silvia would find out he had moved on. He did not plan to keep her from their children, he just needed the smoke to clear.

"Donavan, you can't just take it all away from her like this," said Sanity.

"I am not, sis. Once she calms down, we can establish visitation and that will be that," responded Donavan.

"That's great but what about her life moving forward? She still loves you dearly. She just needed to get herself together and find her long lost sister," pleaded Sanity. She snatched the cigar from his hands.

"You think I wanted to do all of this? My feelings are fucked up too. She didn't think about how fragile I was when she was pressing me for revenge on Jay and disrespecting me. Then she just abandoned her children. You were there, she left and did not call, text, write or email. Who does that to their children? She knows I have mommy issues and never want my children to experience the void of not having a mother."

"Yeah, I called her, and she never answered," said Sanity, having a change in heart.

What type of mother leaves their children and doesn't make contact for several months. Sanity was present for the hard days when the children were missing their mother. It hurt to console them. She even watched them attach to Lydia who was nurturing them, giving them the mother they lost. Donavan left Sanity on the balcony with her thoughts. He knew Silvia would be looking for him but had no idea she was already on the way.

Inside the banquet hall, Skeet sat at one of the tables. He checked his phone and there was still no return call or text from Karen. He knew something was off because she had not checked on her mother. Instead of being upset, Skeet hired a twenty-four-hour live in nurse until Karen returned. A week prior to her disappearance, she confirmed that the baby was Zak's. It hurt Skeet, but he respected her honesty and could move forward if Karen was sure she was ready to move on.

Skeet observed Donavan enter the banquet hall and go straight to his soon-to-be wife. Skeet admired the love they had for each other. He wanted that happiness and would wait for Karen to decide if she would be the one.

His thoughts were disrupted by the sight of Rachel wandering around. Things between them had gotten worse since Janice died. It dawned on Skeet that maybe she saw something. When she slipped out to the garden, Skeet waited a couple minutes before following. When he made it to the garden, he observed her snorting cocaine.

"So, you're back on this ride again I see," spoke Skeet, approaching her.

He handed her a handkerchief for her running nose. Rachel snatched it from him and wiped her nose. "Well, if you witnessed your father strangling the life out of his baby's mother, you would do drugs too."

Skeet moved in closer to speak. He loved his daughter and showed her a great deal of patience, but he would not be a doormat. "Let's be clear, I have seen and done far worse, and it did not drive me to drug dependency. Make this the last time you say anything about what you saw that night. You obviously don't have the mental compacity to process why things happened, so I won't waste my time trying to explain."

Rachel fired back, "Yeah, like Rena, your golden child. I see why you two get along. She's a killer like you."

"Don't make me say it twice, Rachel," spoke Skeet through gritted teeth.

"Don't worry, one thing I am not is a snitch. But why can't I see my mother!" yelled Rachel.

"Because you are dead to her," responded Skeet.

"What! My mother did not want me? She would not care that I was still alive like Stellan?" taunted Rachel.

Skeet lit his cigar. He was tired of handling Rachel gently. Her outbursts were getting out of hand and if she wanted reality, he would give her just that. Either she would build or break from it.

Rachel repeated her question, "Why can't my mother see me? She probably misses me." She began to cry.

"See what I am saying? You are so fragile. I did it to protect you. I was tired of shit happening to you so I made a move that would ensure no one would hurt you again."

"Like always, you have to control everything!" yelled Rachel.

"Rachel, I am tired of this. For almost a year, you have been walking around here on bullshit. You don't want to make anything of yourself, you refuse therapy, you are dependent on drugs, and I know about the naked pictures on the internet. All I did was take you away from a shitty life so no one would hurt you anymore. Yet, you want to go be in the drama. My father always said you don't know what you raised until you raise it. I see you in a new light at this very moment. If you can handle it, I will give you all the information you need. But if you make one wrong move, I will have to treat you like Janice and Stellan," Skeet finished his eyes cold.

Rachel was shocked. It was like her father transformed into the devil before her eyes. She took another line while Skeet watched in disgust, realizing she was weak just like her mother.

"Okay, I am ready, come on spill it," said Rachel, wiping her nose.

"Your mother was a junkie. All she wanted to do was party. I loved her so much and wanted a family with her. When she gave birth to you, I laid out the red carpet only to learn she could not commit to being a mother. When I moved on, she took you to spite me. Under her watch, you were raped by your Aunt Linda's ex-husband. Then she dragged you around from state to state exposing you to several dysfunctional relationships. The nail in the coffin was when Rena's mother tried to kill you about Stellan. When you woke up from your coma, you lost your memory. It was the perfect storm to fake your death," said Skeet, his voice elevated.

Their conversation was disturbed by Sanity. She had been sitting unseen listening to the conversation. "Wow, the men in this family are real pieces of work. I hope my other brother is normal."

"I want to leave this prison, get out in the world, meet my mother," demanded Rachel.

Her words made Skeet angry. He had sacrificed it all for her safety only for her to want to go back to the drama.

"Fine. But leave with only one car and the clothes on your back. I am over this pampered princess shit. You not doing anything productive, just like your mother," said Skeet, turning to walk away.

Sanity stopped him and spoke softly, "No, brother, set your pride to the side. She is still your daughter. You love her, and you are just angry right now. Remember, she is also a part of her mother whether you like it or not. Money is not enough to fill the void of knowing who you are. This world is ugly. Give her a fighting chance out here. You can continue to protect her while she figures things out."

Skeet stood with his back turned, processing his sister's words. She was right, he was wearing his pride on his sleeve. Instead of confirming it, he walked away and returned to the banquet hall to his seat. Instead of thanking her aunt, Rachel barged away. Whether her father gave her money or not she was leaving.

Sanity returned to the party and took a seat at the table with Skeet. She looked around at all the happy guests and beautiful décor. Everything looked so perfect on the surface. It was the greatest deception for those on the outside looking in on the LC Daubs legacy.

Her great grandfather LC Daubs took the first step to build a legacy for his future generations. It skipped to her father Daubs who elevated it and laid a path for his children and grandchildren. Their family did not wear the battle scars he had endured from his mother dying while giving birth to him, the tragic deaths of his aunt and uncle, and his father's suicide. Daubs made sure they had the best of the best and could enjoy life. But under the beautiful layers were dark secrets, trauma, death, and deception. Sanity's mother was in prison, Donavan's mother was dead, Skeet had to grow up without his mother only to get her back for a short time before losing her tragically.

The cycle of control continued. Both Skeet and Donavan were taking their children away from their mothers. Sanity could understand what Rachel was going through. They both needed their mothers to know who they really were. She decided to turn in for the night in one of the guest suites but the text from Silvia made her remember the grand finale would happen that night.

"Hey, Skeet, I need to tell you something," said Sanity.

"No more about Rachel, I won't leave her hanging," responded Skeet, gesturing for her to leave him be.

"That's not it, Silvia is on her way, she just texted me."

"Well, this will be interesting," said Daubs, taking a seat at the table.

For the next hour, they sat at the table watching Donavan and Lydia on the dance floor. It would all come to an end once Silvia arrived.

Finally, Skeet received a security notification on his phone. When he reviewed the video, it was Silvia at the gate. Skeet watched the camera as Silvia made her way to the banquet hall. As she walked, his security scanners could not detect any obvious weapons.

"I think it's time to let Donavan know," said Skeet.

Daubs objected, "No, let's see if he is still quick on his feet."

They both laughed in unison. Sanity rolled her eyes and took a gulp from her bottle. They all three sat and enjoyed what would probably be the last beautiful moments of the night.

After Zak did not answer any calls or use his credit cards for several weeks, Sharae contacted Borya and returned to her home in Tennessee. She knew something was wrong because Zak never went this long without contacting her. She checked all the jails and hospitals that she could think of but came up with nothing.

Then Jay contacted her looking for Zak. After Jay explained all that was going on in Atlanta, Sharae packed up Zia, Zion, Leona, and her youngest son Sion. They traveled to be with Jay and Priest. Now everyone was living together in one of Zak's properties in Buckhead. The house was the first house they purchased after becoming engaged.

Priest was now out of his coma but was burdened with the news that he had full blown AIDs. He was so distracted by making money and looking for Matthew that he ignored the HIV symptoms. At this stage, he was gravely ill and had to stay in the AIDs ward at the hospital. At first, Priest thought he had transmitted the virus from his risky behavior when he was in the cult. But based on the doctor's timeframe of transmission, it was on Jay again.

Over the years, Priest had committed to one woman and that was Jay. He began displaying risky behavior when Matthew went missing and again Jay was always in the room. Jay was tested and was positive for HIV. It was her luck that she was not at AIDs level yet.

Now, both Priest and Matthew resented her because she was always the cause of their suffering. Jay was spending her days fighting the virus, dealing with a son that hated her, and trying to take care of Priest who did not want her around. But she did not complain because she knew she deserved everything they dished out. Now was the time for her to get in tune with her faith. The hospital chapel became her place for peace and serenity.

Matthew despised his mother, but it would not stop him from going with her to the hospital daily. He was young but knew his time with his father was running out. The twelve-year-old was wise beyond his years and his exposure to Daubs had him on a whole other level mentally. He wasn't the average kid that spent their days playing video games, sports, and getting into mischief. His priorities were keeping himself physically healthy and making his father's last days comfortable. He prayed over him multiple times per day, played classical music, and kept fresh plants in his room.

Jay felt like her son was a stranger to her. Matthew was so disciplined and needed minimum attention. He was self-motivated, he read everything, kept his room clean, worked out, ate healthy, and meditated daily. If he was not at the hospital with his father, you could find him at the local dojo in a martial arts class. Jay tried to connect with him, but her efforts were unsuccessful. She knew he would never love her again and she would settle for just being in both of their worlds like Priest was trying to do from the beginning.

It was another day at the hospital. When Jay finished her appointment, she picked up her medications and went straight to Priest's room. When she walked in, Matthew was lying next to his father in the small bed.

Priest's health was declining rapidly. He was hardly coherent, always rambling his mother's name. He told his son that he could see her in the light with her arms out waiting to welcome him. Every day when Matthew arrived, he would ask his father how close he was to his mother. On this day, Priest told him he only had one more step to take. Their moment was disturbed by Jay presence. Irritated, Matthew barged out. He sat in the waiting area until he received the text he was waiting for. He looked in on his parents before going to the stairwell. He went down two levels where Daubs was waiting.

They greeted each other with a warm hug before Daubs spoke, "How are things with your father?"

"He said he is in arms reach of his mother now. He can smell the scent of lavender. I just wish I had this time with him alone instead of sharing him with my mother. I hate her, she is the cause of it all," responded Matthew.

"Son, always remember that death is a part of life. As for your mother, she is rather troublesome," said Daubs.

Matthew stood silent for several seconds. "When my father dies there will be nothing else left here for me. I want to go back to Soring Eagle."

"My son, you will always have a place at Soring Eagle. I will hang around for a few more days just in case you need me."

Daubs exited the stairwell. Matthew returned to the hospital room where his mother was pacing while doctors were examining Priest. Matthew went to his father's bedside.

When the doctors stepped away, Priest used his last ounce of strength to speak, "Son! I love you and I am in my mother's arms now." He closed his eyes and allowed his mother to fully embrace him. The scent of lavender danced in his nose, and he melted in the warmth and softness of his mother's embrace.

"Time of death 11:11am," called the doctor.

Matthew turned and walked past his mother, exiting the room. He went to the elevator where Sharae stopped him.

"Where are you going?" she questioned.

Matthew turned to Sharae. "Thank you for everything. There is nothing left here for me. I am going back home where I belong."

TO BE CONTINUED